D1168558

Rope-Dancer

Also by M. J. Fitzgerald

CONCERTINA

Rope-Dancer

M. J. FITZGERALD

Random House New York

Copyright © 1985 by M. J. Fitzgerald
All rights reserved under International and Pan-American Copyright Conventions.
Published in the United States by Random House, Inc., New York.
Originally published in Great Britain by Pan Books Ltd., London, in 1986.

Library of Congress Cataloging-in-Publication Data

Fitzgerald, M. J.
Rope-dancer.

I. Title.
PS3556.I834R6   1987   813'.54   86-26159
ISBN 0-394-55921-5

Manufactured in the United States of America
98765432   24689753   23456789
First American Edition

FOR MY FATHER

Acknowledgments

I am grateful to Rosalind Belben, Catharine Carver
and Gabriel Josipovici for their encouragement; to Rosalind Belben
for the title *Creases;* to my father for the translations of Virgil
and Ovid in *Eurydice*; and to my editor, T. J. Binding, for his support
and his help in putting the collection together.

The title is taken from the Man Ray painting called
"Rope-Dancer Accompanies Herself with Her Shadows."

Contents

Creases

A man and a woman met and became lovers. She was big and strong, with long lithe limbs, brown eyes that never flinched, a large mouth and hands that could have made a comfortable nest for a bird and its fledglings. He was tall and thin, though not too thin; he 'never felt ridiculous when they walked hand in hand through the spring-singing park. His eyes were green and rather close-set; when he smiled the laughter-lines fanned out to the temples, and the lips stretched across his face like an elastic band. She teased him about his nose, but this was only to balance the painful pleasure of seeing the laughter-lines. She loved him and he was in love with her: in a constant state of excitement, he drove into her almost before the first kiss had passed between them, and no sooner had he been satisfied inside her than he saw the long legs and the brown eyes and felt himself rising once more. She received him and loved him. Sometimes when he had exhausted himself and lay asleep next to her, she would trace with her eyes the thin lines around his eyes and anticipate the moment when he would wake and the smile would bless her with pleasure. Other times his touch along the length of her long body would turn her to a trembling leaf. Until she realised that he did not like her except when still and strong, and she steeled herself and trembled no more.

By summer they found their love was magic: she seemed to have endless powers of transformation, moulding herself to his desire as if she were clay. If he was weary of the long limbs, she watched herself become small and slight for his delight. When weary of her smallness, she grew large breasts into which he buried himself, and when that ceased to satisfy him she became a child and even a man. Only her eyes remained brown and unflinching. She had no wish that he should change, she was content that her transformations should awaken the smile in his eyes and to see the laughter-lines fan out to the temples.

One day he became tired of her. He had to go on a long journey and did not want to take her with him, her eyes made him uneasy and he disliked most the tacit assumption that because she loved him he must somehow love her too. The assumption was his, not hers: he thought she thought they must love each other for ever. She did not think; she knew she loved him and would be all things to him as long as she could see his smile, but the words 'for ever' had no meaning.

He decided to put her away before going on his journey. He had a standard-sized cardboard box into which he put all things that had become useless—blunted pocket-knives, old letters—and he called her to him and asked her to become small enough to go in the box. Joyfully she waited for the change that would bring the smile, but nothing happened. She remained big and strong, lithe-limbed and clear-eyed, until the brown grew misty with puzzlement. He thundered and swore, his brows grew closer above his close-set eyes. He was angry. He ordered her to step inside the box. She curled up in as tight a ball as she could, but her head would not fit, however hard she tried to make herself less bulky. He thundered and swore, ordered her out and told her to strip. She cast her clothing aside and stepped in. He pushed her, pressed down her shoulders; she tried to bury her head, but the eyes and nose still remained above the level of the box and he could not fit the top on. He stamped his feet and ordered her to get out. She stood by the side, looking down, trying to see how he could best be satisfied this time, when he thrust her in head-first. Her forehead hit the bottom and she felt his hands; her left leg he wrapped around the back, with the foot twisted to fit in the groove between the shoulder and neck. Her right leg he fitted below the underside of the thigh and then pushed the buttocks further in. Her arms were curled against her chest and her nose was squashed and twisted against the bottom right-hand corner of the box. Quickly and deftly, as if fixing a set of batteries to a transistor, he fitted the top and took a large elastic band from his desk to secure it shut. He sighed with satisfaction and thought next day he would ask someone to help him carry the heavy box to the attic. He went out to celebrate and brought back a girl who giggled and did not believe him when he claimed the cardboard box that stood in the middle of the room held a woman. Thinking that she might spring out at him if he removed the elastic band he resisted the temptation to prove it.

Inside she was in pain. The left ankle and foot were twisted and the tendons of the leg stretched as if about to snap. The squashed nose brought continuous tears to her eyes, the arms developed pins and needles and the tightly bent knee-joint of her right leg throbbed. She did not move: she wanted to remain there if that was his will and only wished the box had been a little bigger or she could have transformed herself into the small person who would have neatly fitted. For hours, for days, for a lifetime she lay still trying to think of other things to distract her from the pain that from being clearly localised in five places gradually coagulated and invaded her whole cramped body and then spread outward like an oil-spill to the sides of the box and beyond the darkness to the room beyond until the universe itself was pounding with it. She thought he must feel it, it was so dense, or at least hear it as it beat and drummed louder and louder in her ears, but he was merely aware that he had not yet taken the box to the attic, it was still standing in the middle of the room with its top on and the elastic band around it. He had been busy and preoccupied with preparations for the long journey, having to settle his business, sell his house and the car, invest the money to have an income with which to pursue his travels at leisure; and the girl he had brought back turned out to be a nasty bitch who wanted to be paid for every favour but would not move out, lounging around in her black and red underwear and performing sudden and obscene strip-teases to get money from him.

One day, shortly before he left, he got around to moving the box. He asked the girl to help him and because her swinging breasts were finally unable to rouse him, she agreed to, for a sum. They stepped near the box and were about to lift it when the strained elastic gave way and lashed them both in the face, the top flew as far as the ceiling and landed softly on the carpet, and the woman's left leg sprang out. The pain of sudden release was as great as the pain she had been enduring, but it was so different it felt like relief as her right leg followed her left leg, the box toppled sideways and the nose ceased being ground and twisted. She could not move and lay there, in darkness, trembling like a leaf in a strong wind, with her naked limbs exposed. The girl giggled, but the man's brows came closer to his close-set eyes. He was angry; the sight of the exposed flesh made him rise fiercely; when he pulled her out, the face bloated by tears, the deep grooves made by the pressure of the side of the box on her skin made him, briefly, fiercely tender. He smiled at her suddenly, drew her to him, and if her body could not forget the pain, she could, and was happy to see the laughter-lines fan out to the temples.

The girl vanished within the hour, leaving the bedroom littered with underwear and taking some valuable silver that had been in the family for generations.

He could no longer treat her harshly, thrust her back in the box, yet he did not want to take her with him. Her eyes still made him uneasy and besides, she had become uglier, her limbs did not function properly, they occasionally jerked like those of an epileptic, and her long stride had become crab-like and carried them sideways as they walked hand in hand through the spring-singing park.

As he was packing the last of the ancient books he had found at the top of a cupboard, one of them fell open on a diagram-drawing of a crouched man: the buttocks were against ankles and heels, the head touched the knees and the arms were lying back alongside the pleated body. Underneath was written 'FOLDED LEAF'. The man showed the book to the woman and told her to strip again, crawl into the box and arrange herself in the position shown in the diagram. She felt the profoundest terror but was helpless to refuse to do as he wished. She wormed backwards and doubled up. The box was too narrow for her arms to lie back, so she tucked them against her chest. She cupped her face in her hands and looked one last time at the man as he smiled at her, safely away in the box. He put on the top with ease and tied a thick rope around it, to make sure she could not get out. He thought she could not feel pain: the book stated that 'FOLDED LEAF' was a position of rest and very comfortable. And indeed the pain was not excruciating this time. She found she could move slightly, arching her back to take the pressure off her knees and calves, and turning her face from side to side when the neck became too stiff; but after a while there was no real relief from the ache and discomfort. She penetrated deep into it and closed her eyes, thinking that soon he would return and take her out of the box; and she would see the laughter-lines fan out to the temples.

The years went by. The man enjoyed a fruitful journey that made him wealthy and successful. One autumn day as he walked in a wood of chestnut trees in a far country he remembered her eyes and returned. He had trouble finding the box, which he had stored in the attic of the house he had sold. It had been removed with his other belongings to a warehouse, but in transit the label was lost, the box had been shunted from one part of the warehouse to another and finally buried under large shabby trunks and sofas and chairs and cupboards that belonged to a couple with little money and many children. The man spent a lot on the warehouse keepers to find the cardboard box. Finally it was retrieved, battered and damp, sagging where the foot of a sofa had been resting. The man took it to the large house he had made his home, and because he could not lift it, asked the taxi-driver to put it down in the master bedroom. His hands shook like the hands of an old man while he undid the various knots, and his heart-beat took his breath away when he removed the top. She crouched still as a folded leaf, with her hands cupping her face and her eyes shut. He tore away the cardboard all around her and wrapped her nakedness in the warm goose-down blanket from the bed. For days he massaged her to straighten her limbs, until she lay on the floor, her hands by her side, her legs stretched out, the body bruised and permanently puckered and pleated.

She did not open her eyes again, but one day the man got her to move and led her, her hand in his, through the spring-singing park.

Perspective on the First You

Remember when we went to Ireland? How cold it was. Your eyes, your eyes haunt me my love, and the way you have of turning around always looking over your left shoulder and your eyes when you turn, your eyebrows your nose lips the lines around your eyes on your forehead. The back of your neck: you were mine not because we made love in and out of bed, in and out of season, but because as we drove, as we sat, as we walked, I could raise my hand and touch the back of your neck and feel the soft flesh beneath the hairline, the two vertical tendons taut even when you were relaxed asleep in the small double bed at the boarding-house in Kilnacloona.

Rain darkened the earth, the low sky pressed us to the ground, kept us in our bed to play the most silent of games; at nightfall green and grey lights and shadows chasing each other over the hills on the horizon and we walked in the after rain, and in the spring we went to Exmoor and walked through woods carpeted with blue-bells, lay on the hillside kept soft and springy by the transformation of sheep's droppings into earth. We listened to their bells and watched giant clouds; I wanted to play at seeing shapes in the clouds but it was too late, the silence had grown and could not be broken.

Is there no way? There is no way, it's hopeless, it isn't working you said love me less you said. How does one love less? Will it end my love my love; yes you said. It's always worse the first time you said, being in love. No one's died of a broken heart you said. I can't breathe without you, I'll die—don't be so melodramatic you said. Come back to me my love my love It'll be all right you said, you'll find someone else you said, let me go you said I can't breathe with you around. Go I said I give you eight months you said You'll marry have a dozen kids. I'll die I said—don't be so melodramatic you said It'll be okay it's always worse the first time being in love you said.

Remember the first time you touched me?

We were climbing up a bank, he had come to visit me and we had gone for a walk, one of those long leisurely strolls we used to take.

We were climbing up this bank, it was rather steep; remember, you were in the middle of saying something, I was ahead of you? You put out a hand to help me in the climb: low in my back, below the waist, where the scar is. There was nothing to it, your hand was simply there, helping me. I didn't feel anything apart from the pressure of the hand pushing me slightly, helping me move forward. There was no interruption to your words; but there must have been something more because I have not forgotten it.

Of course we had touched, shaken hands before, I had even put my arm through his in happy companionship: we were friends.

We were friends. Words tumbled out of us as if time was not long enough to tell all we had to say. We were friends, eager to see each other, content to be apart. We met each other's friends and your day-to-day life had become part of me. The pleasure lost is in the small things, how you would tell me that the rattle of the window had kept you awake and I would tell you how the cat had decided to sleep in the airing cupboard and how she had woken in the middle of the night and started miaowing and scratching the door to be let out. We phoned each other once, sometimes twice a week, and spoke of who had come to dinner, which of our friends we had seen and what plays, what films, what concerts we had been to. We shared the books we read. We gossiped; we told each other which of our friends had broken with whom, who was going out with whom, how so and so was in poor shape and so and so in better shape than we had seen him or her for months. Little daily things: our lives were full of each other's life.

The weekend you came to stay it was all as it had been for months except for the touch. You even slept on the mattress on the floor by my bed because the sitting-room was taken up by other visitors, remember?

How did it happen? We were such good friends. It wasn't until months later. Was it because we had not seen each other for a while? When we finally organized to meet and I was waiting for him in the buffet at the station—a short meeting between trains, you said you had too much work—I remember I found it difficult to breathe, as if a thick band had been tightened around the lungs: the classic symptom. With you? Of all people, with you? Of all the boys that came and went, with him, my friend? I didn't think of it like that then, I didn't know: I was just conscious of tightness from jaw to crotch, an eagerness to see him that was almost fear.

You leant over, gave me a light kiss on the cheek and smiled; the tightness went and everything returned to normal, except that a few minutes later I wanted to stretch out my hand and touch the sleeve of your jacket. A few minutes after that, just before you had to leave, just as you turned your head to call the waiter, I wanted to touch the back of your neck. The tightness returned as we kissed and shook hands; you were irritated when I suggested another meeting, but agreed; then you cancelled it, but phoned the next day, said you were going and would I like to drive to Norfolk with you, stay somewhere, go for long walks, do some bird-watching, just a couple of days.

We didn't talk much during the drive in the Fiat, remember how it felt and sounded as if we were sitting on top of the engine? It was a sudden strain to talk, I had to breathe deeply to breathe at all—and I don't know, somehow everything no longer seemed important enough, no longer worth telling you, as if there was something overwhelming that should be said if we could find the words. You turned to me at one point, smiled and apologized. You were very tired you said and weren't going to be very good company and would I bear with you. I put my hand on your sleeve then: like his touch so many months before, my hand was on his sleeve and somehow it was the most important thing in the world and removing it seemed impossible, although I did remove it, I did turn away, I did look out of the window at the flat East Anglian landscape . . . the band squeezed me tighter from jaw to crutch, belly, lungs, breasts, kidneys, liver, heart. I could not breathe.

A little later I told you I didn't feel well, could we stop a minute, have a brief walk. You were worried, remember? I opened the door, leant out breathing deeply. You insisted I bend over, put my head low, in between my legs, breathing in and out steadily, one-two, three-four; one-two, three-four. You walked around, went into the field, I think he had a pee, you returned, put your hand on my head, are you feeling better you said; yes I said. You ruffled my hair, cut too short, like a soft brush you told me once, twice, a few times. Okay then you said, shall we go on; yes I said. As you started the car I thought I am in love.

And then a chant an incantation a prayer: I love you I love you I love you. Breathing in I love, breathing out you. The exhalation, a you that contained every moment of his past, every inch of his body, every nook and cranny of his being, what I knew of you and what I would never know, the friend and stranger you were, the words and the silence, what we could not share as well as what we did.

We took separate rooms, of course: the man at the desk leered at us, knowing more than either of us did, reducing already whatever might have happened to the secretive life of his imagination. The tightness had gone, exorcised by the magic words. I felt light-headed, extraordinarily light-headed, as one does on top of high mountains, breathing rarefied, dizzying air. I didn't want to tell you, not yet. I would savour it, sing it to myself for a little longer, then speak. I had no doubts you felt the same, no doubts at all.

There were only three possible words between us then, and the silence pressed down on us like the dank heat of an August day.

We were walking side by side—the evening was cloudy, it was threatening rain—when he turned to me and said he wanted to make love. Like that, I want to make love to you and then my name. You always emphasize the 'i' differently from anyone else, as if it were an excuse to smile I thought. I've never made love I said. I know you said. I love you I said. I know you said (how? I had not known until a couple of hours before). Do you love me I said. I don't know you said, I want to make love to you. I don't know I said. What you said. Make love I said. The tightness from jaw to crotch. I feel as if I'm being squeezed by a python I said. You laughed: it's roughly what I'd like to do you said. Oh do you love me I said. I don't know you said. I don't know that I know the meaning of the word he said, months later. Then it started to rain and he took my hand and we ran back to the hotel, as in a television ad for milk chocolates, except that neither of us is beautiful, my run is breast-heavy and his almost a mince. No I said as we came through. No what you said. No I said. All right you said, don't look so frightened. No I said. I smiled and you smiled and the tightness went. You kissed me on the cheek outside my room and the tightness returned worse than ever before. Yes I said. No you said. I love you I said. I want you you said. All right I said. Do you think really you said. Yes I said. No, I think we better not you said. But I love you I said. I know you said. You kissed me and you shut the door and left me in my room alone.

The man at the desk leered the next morning. I told you I wished he had something to leer about and you laughed: you aren't that romantic after all are you you said. No I said. Shall we give him something to leer about you said and stretched out your hand and touched my cheeks and then my lips. You're blushing you said, laughing. Yes I said, you've never done that before. I've wanted to you said. Oh I said. For a long time you said. I didn't know what to say: really I said. Yes months, about a year now. No I said, we were friends. Yes you said, that's why I didn't tell you. Oh, I said, I hadn't realized. Yes, I know you hadn't, you are very young. Don't say that I said, remember? Sitting at the breakfast table, the cold sunny day ahead of us, all clouds blown away by the night wind (did the wind rattle the window so he could not sleep? I didn't ask. I could no longer talk: whether we touched or not lust was between us, demanding, suffocating us, destroying the friendship, eating into it by every abstention from each other's body as much as by each taste. Whether we made love or not, it was over, we could never be friends again. Every time we came near, it would intrude, tightening its grip from jaw to crotch, blocking the mind except for the whimper, the miaow of a kitten left to suffocate in an airing cupboard. Whether he touched me or not, there was no relief, no lasting relief. Nothing helped.)

We made love that afternoon. After we talked a little, but it was as if words had lost their meaning—no, as if they were too distant approximations, as if I would have to speak all the words in all the languages to come anywhere near the meaning of our two bodies lying on the same bed, my head on his shoulder, his right hand holding my left breast. Then he fell asleep and I lay counting the grey hairs on his chest. When he woke he made love again violently, briefly, silently. I told him later that I felt as if I was wrapped in swaddling clothes, tightly contained, pressed down, unable to breathe. You laughed, you kissed me. I want you again you said.

The man at the desk had something to leer at now, and though we were unable to talk to each other, it was all right then, our bodies talked for us, seemed to talk for us. It was later that talking became more important, that our bodies could not longer keep up the pretence of talk, and only the permanent tightening and trembling of the body at his touch remained, only the constant listless nervousness when we were apart. I could no longer be content at being apart, and I was not content when we were together. More, more, more. More of what though? Our bodies had drunk of each other, we were drunk with each other. More? What more? The less would have been the more. We lacked words. Those precious daily words I could no longer speak, how is the work going, what did you do yesterday, what shall we do tomorrow, have you read this book, let's see this film, did you hear that programme on the radio, watch this programme on television; not what do you think, do you think of me, do you love me what do you think what are you thinking a penny for your thoughts are you tired of me are you bored do I bore you make love to me make love with me love me love me. What are you thinking. Talk to me tell me something.

Did the wind rattle the window so you could not sleep don't go away, don't leave me I need you.

You are stifling me, I can't breathe with you around he said.

I can't breathe without you around me, without you inside me I thought, I could not say.

Let me go he said. The 'i' was shorter, he did not smile.

Okay go I said. No don't please don't I thought. Go, go, go I said. I can't breathe without you I thought. It will be all right he said, you'll find someone else. Yes I say, of course I say and he left. No one's died of a broken heart he said. I can't breathe without you I thought. And he left. Let me go he said. The 'i' was shorter, as everyone else pronounces my name, without a smile. Yes I say, go I say. But I can't breathe without you I said. It'll be okay he said, there'll be someone else, you'll marry, have a dozen kids. It's always worse the first time he said, being in love. Yes I say. Will I fall in love again I said. He laughed: I give you eight months, at most a year. Oh I said, as much as that I said. Well perhaps less. Eight months without breathing I thought. I'll die I said. Don't be so melodramatic he said.

No I say, all right. Can we be friends I say. We are he says. No I say. Of course we are he says. Yes of course we are I say.

Falling Sickness

The window where she sat and watched the world go by, framed
a view of valley, lake and blue mountains, and gave on to a large
irregular square. She leant forward on her chair, her arms folded
on the sill, and took pleasure in this child's grin, that girl's way of
hopscotching, a boy's long-legged awkwardness; delighted in a
couple whose hands brushed absent-mindedly as they sat side by
side on the bench, and another couple who turned and smiled at
each other. Even before the first time she fell, she had seen an
extraordinary man, with the kind of demanding beauty that seemed
to ask of her that she should leap after him: she had stood poised
at the window, her hands grasping the frame, ready to jump if he
as much as turned to look in her direction, but although he remained
in the square and was busy and concerned with the life around
him, he seemed totally unaware of the plump figure teetering on
the ledge; and soon she was tumbling in her first fall.

She rolled down a slope, laughing, enjoying the quick changes
from sky to grass as her head spun, hit the occasional stone that
jutted out and was stopped in her fall by the upward slope of the
facing hill. Bruised and elated, she lay, aware of the crackling grass,
the hum of insect life just beyond her ear. Behind it was an intense
silence: after a few minutes it worried her. She rose on her elbows
to see if he was there who had said the words and had seemed to
be falling with her, and saw she was alone. He must have rolled
away from her, he would surely find her; it was best to remain
where she was and wait. She relaxed back and dozed, content, until
ants began to ticle her bare legs, a spider bit her cheek and she had
to move her head constantly to stop large flies from settling on
mouth and eyes.

What compelled her to begin the long trek back that first time
was the hope, the near certainty that she would meet him on the

way back. She thought of the possibilities: he had been stopped by some hillock; unlike her, perhaps he had not been able to enjoy the fall and had succeeded in grasping the branch of a low tree or bush to prevent himself falling further; anyway, he was waiting for her.

She looked around the small valley surrounded by low hills, conquered the lassitude that invaded her at the idea of moving and set out to find a path. She searched along the foot of the hill she had tumbled down, with no success: in fact she began to doubt that could possibly have been the one, it seemed so steep and forbidding to her upturned gaze. The facing hill on the other hand was pleasantly sloped, although when she began to climb through the stubble she found it was a mass of thistles and nettles. Before long her legs were so scratched and swollen she found it difficult to walk. There didn't seem to be an end to the wild growth on all sides. The only thing she could see to do was fold herself into a ball, hoping her dress would protect her a little, roll back to the foot of the hill and begin the search for a path.

—When I get back I shall practise soft landings,—she thought as she landed hard on the small of her back. The clothes had been no protection, the whole skin surface stung painfully.

While the nettle-sting throbbed and her back remained rigid with pain she played games: she counted the leaves on branches of a beech tree close by, and the blades of grass level with her eyes; she tried to see more blades without turning her head, until her eyes ached, and hoped the sky would become spattered with clouds so she could count them, but it remained a deep relentless blue. Eventually she began moving her limbs, tentatively, fearful of what movement might reawaken.

—Not too bad—she said and heaved herself on her feet. Blood had streaked her legs and arms but was now coagulated, the nettle-sting had subsided, the back only ached if she bent at a certain angle. Now to find a path.

She searched for months: there seemed no way out, any track she found and followed led to impenetrable walls of thorns. She walked the length and breadth of the valley countless times, walked around each hill, saying to the silence that what comes down must go up, ridiculous that there should be no way out—.

For long periods she lay in the grass counting branches, leaves, bushes; insects, ants; telling herself that when she had counted one million she would begin looking again; that when she had counted one million she would brace herself and worm her way through any one of the paths, regardless of thorns and nettles. It took her years to build up courage: she dreaded pain.

While she counted the first million, his words frequently returned to her mind, making her heart jump; but by the time she took determined steps through the wild undergrowth she had forgotten why she wanted to leave the valley. Although, as she began the scramble, having suddenly recalled a childhood lesson that if nettles are grasped firmly they sting less, she remembered vividly sitting at her window watching the world go by. In the end it was the memory of that pleasure that kept her going throughout the tedious and uncomfortable way that wound interminably round countless hills: at times she had to crawl on all fours, at times slither on her belly; she spent many hours pinching her skin to remove the more superficial thorns, and licking the scratches when she could not find streamlets in which to bathe. It remained almost intolerably hot, and her discomfort was made worse by flies drawn by the smell of blood. Once she met a goat who helpfully chewed a narrow path for a few miles, and twice the thick growth opened out into a clearing of spring grass through which she walked for some days, on the second occasion in the company of a stag that appeared suddenly and as suddenly disappeared just as the clearing closed into wilderness. The interludes made the necessity of forging a way through the undergrowth all the worse: the newly healed scratches bled again and became criss-crossed with a new crop, and fresh thorns embedded themselves on top of thorns that had gone too deep to be prised out.

At the top she mounted a stud and returned to the window. Many years had passed: she remembered the grin of the child in the girl who walked by holding hands with a young man whom it took her a while to recognize as the long-legged adolescent. Couples carried babies; the man was at the other end of the square, talking to an attentive crowd. She leant forward with a sigh of relief, trying to hear what he said. But he was too far.

*

The second time she fell was strange: the door opened, she turned, he said it's me; she smiled, feeling quite safe, having forgotten the first fall though her back still ached occasionally and her skin felt tender at times with the memory of nettles and thorns. She hoped he would join her at the window, where she was still straining to hear what was being said at the other end of the square. Instead he said:

—Give me your address then—and she was pitched in an exhilarating headlong flight that lasted a second. She thought:

—Should have practised soft landings—hit the bottom and doubled up: there wasn't an inch of her that did not hurt. She rocked for weeks, moaning should've jumped.

When the cold became the worse pain, she raised herself on her knees. He would not be there, she knew she had fallen too fast, too far. Sheer rock, dotted here and there with straggly bushes, tilted towards her when she looked up. She couldn't see the top.

—What do I do now?—she thought, and knelt back to remember the wonderful flight and the way he had said give me your address then. She wondered whether she could stay there, but it was too cold.

—Last time it was better—she thought.

—At least it was hot—she thought and rubbed her bruised arms to keep the circulation going.

—Must find a way out of here—she concluded as her teeth began to chatter.

She was in the dry bed of a river, flanked by high rocks, and thought that if she walked either way she should eventually come out. But within hours tall rocks dammed both ways. She hunted along the whole length of the ravine for the lowest ledge of rock which could give her a handhold, leapt on her short legs to try and reach it, looked for a stone to make a step; but the nearest ledge was more than three feet beyond her reach, and the rock that would have made a tall enough step was beyond her strength to carry or push.

When dark fell, she crouched against the ravine, numb with cold, until a stag lifted her on its antlers, set her on the ledge and, warmed by its breath, she slept.

The following months were a slow, painful ascension, gripping at little protrusions in the rock, heaving herself from one inch to the next, frequently slithering back a foot at a time. During the day goats disturbed dust and fragments of rock that came hurtling down on her upturned face; stared at her, chewing, and scampered off loosening a further shower of debris. At night, terrified by the howl of wolves yet comforted by their presence, she clung to the rock-face when the ledge was not wide enough for her to lie with her face against the biting wind.

She never dared look down for fear of her desire: falling had been so exhilarating, the memory of it was a temptation to let go, and only the knowledge that if she fell the excitement would be followed by a worse pain than the discomfort of bleeding hands and feet, and aching shoulders, kept her climbing. She had completely forgotten the window.

When she reached the top she was in the square: the man was standing alone looking at the house. She thought—now would be the time—but felt too weary to run, tap him on the shoulder, say here I am. By the time she had walked across he had been dragged away, smiling, by a crowd of children, amongst whom she recognized the two boys of the couple who had turned and smiled at each other. She returned to the window beyond which the world continued to go by and slept with her head in her folded arms.

*

When she woke she thought—just in case—and began to train herself to fall on a large mattress she placed in a corner of the room, watching how a cat she fed with choice pieces of meat twisted its body to land when she threw it from the top of a tall ladder. She endeavoured to imitate the movement and spring to the ground on her toes and the tips of her fingers. She sacrificed many hours of window-watching to her fear of the pain, but it was no use. She had time to ask:

—If I were to fall, would you cath me?—

—No—he said and as she reeled and freewheeled through the air she told him

—Well, that's honest of you—relaxed completely and shut her eyes: she was going to enjoy the fall at least; she was well-trained, it wouldn't hurt. Then she hit water, gasped and gulped as she sank, and surfaced to flounder in a green sea.

—What will they think of next—she yelled, and took a mouthful of water.

—This is too much—she added and cried for the first time. But crying made her drink, the water tasted of mud, her clothes were dragging her down. She stripped in a wild jig and began a breast-stroke that resembled the anxious paddling of a mongrel. Her breath ran out, the effort of keeping her mouth above water strained unused muscles; she trod water; she swam. She became unable to take the deep breaths she needed.

—I wonder how long I can last—she thought at last, treading water: she wasn't sure whether any time had passed and imagined she had remained stationary in the middle of an unchanging sea, an unchanging sky; the ache in her shoulders and arms could simply be the strain of keeping afloat. She remembered striking water, but nothing on the horizon indicated any progression, any movement; ripples moved out from her and flattened themselves on the surface within seconds. She could be a day's swim from one shore, a year from another, an hour from another, and no signs to point the way she should go. She looked at the sun, it remained midday; she scanned the sky for birds, examined the water for currents, dived unsuccessfully for the short spells her breath allowed to see if she could reach the sea-bed; though sea it was not, the water was green and mud-sweet pond water, and emptier than a desert below a colourless sky.

—Last time it was better—she decided, remembering the inch-by-inch climb, the achievement of aiming for a certain distance and attaining it.

She swam; she trod water; she swam. Time did not pass, the horizon remained a drawn unbroken line, her skin wrinkled, soft-ened and began to work loose from the muscles.

—Should I just let go?—she wondered: it was difficult, her arms and legs moved automatically, if slowly, to keep her afloat. She could not sink.

—I wonder why?—she thought, turned over and swam on her back.

—I'll play dead—she decided, and lay almost submerged with

her eyes shut, spluttering occasionally, waving her arms a little, beating the water with her feet.

—I am lost—she thought.

—If I had jumped I would not have fallen—she concluded as the sun beat down on her closed eyelids and created a dance of coloured gnats.

When she opened them she saw trees swaying in a high breeze. She turned over on her belly to swim, but her feet squelched in mud, and she walked out of the water where the stud waited to carry her back to the window: as it galloped away she looked back and saw an almost perfect circle of trees reflected in the green pond.

*

To prevent herself falling again she closed the shutters of the window and lay in half-darkness on the mattress, thinking of the child whom she had seen with a woman wheeling a toddler in a pushchair, whose grin resembled her mother's, the woman in high-heeled sandals talking to the one who had been the long-legged adolescent; of the fragile couple sitting side by side on the bench, looking around expectantly, and of the man who had not been there but for whom everyone was waiting: the square was dressed in banners and green branches.

—It is too late to jump—she thought when she heard the crowd cheering, turned over on her side to escape the thin shafts of light through the shutters and block some of the noise, and rocked almost imperceptibly.

—Too late, too late, too late.—

*

He said:

—Go on, I'll catch you—and she fell again. And when he found her, her body had rotted in the damp from the undergrowth, where the sun never reached. He remained with her, and she felt the warmth of his body next to her. At last she turned to him:

—Perhaps the fall is the same as the jump.—

—Yes—he said, and freed her hair from the brambles that had become tangled in it.

A Landscape
with Walls

Ever since Briony had discovered the peculiar pleasure of a man's
touch, she was unable to resist the smallest and most timid pass:
her whole body turned towards the one who had laid a glance or
a hand on her and she opened with the abandon of the earth
responding to the sun in spring. She was considered promiscuous
and in winter she agreed.

She was in bed with the 456th man when she realized she was also
picking up bricks that were lying around. She paused and the man
asked what was the matter. Nothing, she said and moaned to please
him: he came and lay helpless on top of her. She thought, helpless,
and came. They lay until he turned over and fell asleep after kissing
the tips of her fingers; she was very sleepy.

The next time Briony caught herself running, slightly out of
breath, as if against time, picking up bricks. She put them in a
large stiff leather apron she was wearing, six or seven as she could
carry no more, scrambled up a bank, dropped the bricks on the
ground and ran back to gather another load. After she had collected
two apronfuls and dropped them where the original pile was, she
began to lay them one on top of the other. No cement, she thought
and came; the man didn't. They lay quiet awhile and then started
again. The bricks were exactly where they had been and she was
laying them one on top of the other. Briony carefully didn't think
no cement in case she should come, but the man soon did, she
stopped and could barely remember what she'd been doing within
a minute or two. They got up and had a cup of tea before he left
to meet a client at the Ritz and she prepared to go out: she needed
a new dress.

In the cafeteria a man looked at her and offered to pay for the coffee and the chocolate cake. They went to his house. Briony fled down the fire-escape before his wife came back with the children, and laughed with delight as she crossed the street: a good lay. And she had laid no bricks.

The third time she slept with the 456th man, who was called Daile and worked as a stockbroker in the City, the bricks were still there. She wore the same apron of stiff dark leather and knew she had to collect more. She ran hither and thither in a bleak black and white landscape that resembled the sets of the Val Lewton films she had been watching in a retrospective on television.

There were hundreds and Briony, with a great feeling of urgency, tried to collect as many as she could. She ran and scrambled, collecting and returning with an apronful of six or seven to the place where she had started to build, and dropping them in a growing pile. In order to be able to go on she told herself as she returned with her fourth load: another ten. But she came as she thought, and the bricks fell from her apron far from where they should have been. Daile had come too: a rare simultaneous orgasm and Briony hadn't noticed. It troubled her and she decided to stop making love with him. She told him she was going on a cruise to the West Indies and wrote to Telecom that her number seemed to be frequently used by men who thought she was a call-girl. They were very kind, within a few days her number had been changed.

Briony was having a meal with the 468th man when Daile came into the restaurant with a woman. He looked at her, she remembered how he had kissed each fingertip so they slipped away from their partners. In bed later the landscape waited for her. This time though she noticed that wherever she looked to right and left, she was surrounded by brick walls. She climbed one, tottering dangerously, and looked around. Each wall was about six feet high and four feet wide, and they extended as far as the eye could see. They weren't really walls, the bricks were not cemented, merely laid one on top of the other. Briony slithered down just in time before the whole six-foot construction toppled over; she would have to build it up again. She was so engrossed in laying bricks that only eventually did she become aware of the body shuddering on top of her. She thought, helpless, but didn't come. She thought, no cement. Nothing. The first time she hadn't for as long as she could remember, it was distressing. Daile looked at her and they started again. The landscape thrust itself at her, she was compelled to go on laying the bricks and she succeeded in re-erecting almost all the wall before they gave up and he fell into an exhausted sleep. Briony put her head on his chest and followed the heart-beat: in the dream she was dancing to its beat, carrying bricks to finish the wall; but she didn't reach it because he turned away from her to lie on his side.

The last time she and Daile made love Briony unsuccessfully tried to take off the leather apron. She refused to run, or kneel and crouch on her haunches to lay one brick on top of the other, but stood very still in the Val Lewton landscape looking at the walls: there seemed to be shadows skulking behind many of them. She opened her eyes, looked at Daile who was looking at her, and finally came again.

One day, as Briony was in bed with the 480th man, who was called Nailen, she was scrambling up one of the walls, behind which there was a figure. She had to see who it was: it had been peering from behind for years. But when she looked over there was no one there. She lost her foothold, landed hard on her back and was covered by a shower of bricks as the man on top of her came. She was badly bruised and couldn't come.

Another time, as she was laying a brick flush with the others and carefully arranged on top of the portions of two bricks underneath, she knew someone was behind the wall nearest her, peering at her over the top. She leapt to her feet and ran to it; she couldn't look around the side, she had to climb and by the time she had managed to get a handhold, then a foothold and hoist herself up, there was no one there, whoever or whatever it was, was a shadow behind the next wall. Gingerly she climbed down and set back to work until Nailen shuddered and she lost the walls and the landscape.

Nailen liked going to bed with her more than the other 479 men had, more than Daile even. But Briony had to make walls; she packed her apron and ran hither and thither, backwards and forwards to have a pile to make into a wall, and when she told him that while they made love she was making walls, he said what a shame because he liked her and left. Briony carefully didn't think and went on a long holiday during which she was laid by 99 men, made no walls and forgot all about it except that occasionally she would wake from a dream of figures skulking behind walls, peering at her and childishly hiding and running away. It wasn't until she went to bed with the 579th man, a diplomat to the exotic tropical island where she was living, that she returned to the Val Lewton landscape and to the compulsive task of collecting bricks to make walls. She thought afterwards as he lay asleep on his back with his dark hair stuck to his forehead with sweat and his arm holding her still against his chest so she could hear the regular beat of his heart, that she should leave the island, and she traced the outline of his eyebrows with her finger before moving away. But he woke and looked at her, and soon she was running hither and thither, scrambling urgently, to make another wall.

Dyle and Briony made love more often than she had ever made love before, perhaps because the island was small, there weren't many problems and Dyle's job was dull. There was little time and less opportunity for her to be laid by anyone else, and after a while she found that she had apparently collected all the bricks there were around: she spent some time hunting the landscape, searching every corner, looking behind every bush and dwarf tree, examining the base of every wall for stray bricks, walking miles and miles from one wall to the next and around each one in her search, until the whole landscape was clean, with walls rising six foot high and four foot wide all around her, as far as the eye could see, and, she knew now, well beyond where the eye could see. She stood in her apron wondering what her next task was until the familiar shudder dispelled the landscape, she thought I'll never see it again, and came for the first time. Dyle kissed the hollow of each elbow and laughed.

*

A long time later she returned. The landscape hadn't changed, there were no bricks lying around, and the walls stood clean and

dark against the black and white set. Briony walked in her leather
apron that felt new and stiff, wondering what she should do. She
felt no urgency now, merely a sense of dullness, almost boredom.
She was certain the walls hid someone: perhaps she should be trying
to discover who? She walked, casting a glance around each wall as
she passed, knowing that whoever or whatever it was could play
hide and seek with her for ever. When the 800th man came and
the scene vanished, Briony remained thoughtful. Unlike the
previous times she had inhabited the place, this time she remembered it vividly. As the man slept with his back towards her, she
puzzled, but it wasn't until the third time that she realized the only
thing she could do was to demolish the walls. She thought, that's
why there's no cement and came for the last time.

Where there had been urgency in the building, there was now a
dull but dogged determination in the destruction. Where there had
been erratic enthusiasm that had led her to make walls wherever
she happened to find herself and bricks had been at hand, there
was now a methodical organization. If she found herself in a maze
of walls, she sought the way to where she had been before, and
continued her task where it had been left off: it was the only way
to defeat the hiding figure.

One night she woke alone in the king-size bed. She had been
lifting and casting aside bricks in her dream, and from then on she
could do it anywhere and at any time. In fact she discovered that
the task seemed lighter, less burdensome, if she was alone. Although
there were still times when a man looked at her and she opened
like the earth in spring, she preferred solitude and became convinced
that once the landscape was free of walls the shadow whose presence
she felt and who she knew was observing her from behind the next
wall, always the next wall, would emerge. Then she would really
be free and would no longer need to walk the place.

But there were so many: thousands more than she had made,
they extended and went on and seemed to multiply so that when
Briony thought she was nearing the end, the next time the horizon
seemed to have been pushed further back and countless more stood
silent and black against the white set.

Walking in a country of olive trees and farms one day, she saw a granary constructed in a way she had never seen before: at each level the cement had been put only at the two ends of each brick, and the wall made into a beehive of intermittent bricks that let the air into the granary. Briony felt a shiver go up her spine: she could see into the granary, beyond to the opposite wall and through it to the olive trees and vines beyond. She sat in the afternoon sun with her back to the granary and walked her landscape. Instead of painstakingly removing brick after brick to demolish the walls, she had merely to remove as many at each level as would prevent anything from hiding behind. She started at the base of the next wall, pushing one brick sideways and then thrusting it out of position: it wasn't easy, and because the construction was not cemented, the whole wall swayed, but Briony persisted and made gaps at every level. When she had finished she could see through clearly and danced with delight: she would confront the figure before long. She opened her eyes and saw a man looking at her through a gap in the granary. Briony smiled, opened to him and laughed to feel and see again a man shuddering helplessly on top of her against a darkening sky. He was the 999th man, hardly more than a boy; his name was Neyde and his father owned the granary.

They made love in the fields and only in the interstices of time, when he wasn't searching her like a mysterious dwelling whose every corner and fold he must know, did she continue her labour. She wondered sometimes that they were so solid: not one wall fell as she removed the bricks.

After a while she gazed through the gaps in one wall to the wall beyond and a framed vista that stretched far into the distance; and suddenly, as she slid one more brick sideways to push it out of position, she saw a man's hand: long-fingered and familiar. Briony remembered Daile taking her hands into his and kissing each fingertip before falling asleep, cried out Daile Daile and leapt to her feet to gaze through the wall, but he had gone. She opened her eyes to dispel the desolation and watched Neyde walking towards her across the vine grove. As they made love the landscape intruded, and Briony stooped, got up, walked through the vines holding his hand, unable to explain, and insistently thrust the next brick out of position and slid it to the ground. She saw the familiar thick-set shoulders and short back and cried Nailen Nailen, but before she had even time to move to the side of the wall and confront him, he had gone and she saw only his shadow pass behind the next wall.

The next day she and Neyde made love for the first time in the small bed at her hotel, as a storm chilled the summer air and darkened the room: she knelt and looked through the brick frame knowing that the next vision would be of Dyle's smile. And indeed so it was. His face was suddenly there, and she could thrust her hand through the gap and trace with her fingers the beautiful arch of his eyebrows. But she would lose the smile. So she looked at him and as he looked at her he became Nailen and Daile by turns. Finally she had no need to open her eyes to see Neyde, who looked at her from every gap in the bricks, until his gaze became that of a stranger and walls and landscape vanished.

The Game

She woke in the middle of the night with the memory of a dream slipping away from her so fast she only caught the sensation. She had been playing chess; she did not remember, but knew she had been White; something had been about to happen.

Rita lay in the dark puzzling; she had not played for years. When had the last time been? Unaccountably wide awake, barely aware of her husband's sleep-breathing next to her, she tried to remember: a picture of the elaborate chess-set on the drawing-room table at home when she was a child rose to the surface of her mind, as clearly defined and detailed as objects in certain paintings, buoyed on a mass of light.

But she had not played then, it was something the boys did: Marcus had been enthusiastic for a while, until stamp-collecting and rugby had taken over; Benjamin, her twin brother, had appeared less enthusiastic and more obsessive. A vivid intaglio arose in Rita's mind's eye of Benjee's rather ugly childish face bent over the set, then his short-fingered, black-nailed hand moving slowly, hovering over a piece, placing it in a new position and the slow grey eyes lifting from the board and looking into the face of an invisible opponent.

She stared at the tableaux from the past: what was the expression in his eyes? But as she stared the picture lost its clarity, became blurred and Rita sighed as she felt herself drifting into sleep. She turned towards her husband's back and wrapped her long thin body around his; he moved his head slightly and murmured, seemed to wake as he turned over and took her in his arms. Rita whispered his name, but he didn't reply: still asleep. She lay still and tried to remember her dream until she was overtaken by another.

'Rita, Rita, wake up.'

She woke to the feel of her husband's face over her.

'Are you awake?'

Her 'yes' contained a strange sob that woke her completely.

'You've been crying in your sleep. What were you dreaming?'

'I don't know.'

She had been playing chess: she was White and something was about to happen.

'Are you all right?'

'Yes. Thanks for waking me. I can't remember it, but it can't have been very pleasant if I cried.'

'Are you okay?'

'Yes, of course, don't worry.'

Rita gave her husband a kiss and snuggled up to him. He held her tightly for a minute, relaxed and was asleep. Rita smiled—he fell asleep like a child.

Then she suddenly saw a chess-board. It was extremely vivid: Black was aligned aggressively, beautifully arranged on the board.

Rita could see it so clearly she began to memorize the position of the various pieces, but a thought interfered and the chess-board began to blur. Whose move was it? She could still see the symmetry of the attack: Black king protected by pawns, one knight and a bishop, and a pyramid arrangement of pieces preventing White's move.

It faded. Whose move was it? If she could have gone on remembering, she would have worked it out. Black attacking so forcefully? White can't have been a very good player. Rita began to drift towards sleep again, and as it overtook her she murmured: 'Benjee.'

The piercing alarm of the clock dispelled dreams and sleep. Ian grunted and reached to switch it off. Silence.

'Don't fall asleep again.'

Rita spoke to her husband.

'No, I won't,' he muttered and grunted.

She lay for a minute or two feeling that what she had just been dreaming and forgotten had been important, that it had contained some revelation she would now never realize, then rose and drew the curtains.

'I think I dreamt of Benjee.'

She spoke standing against the light, framed by the window, naked, tall and thin.

'Is that why you cried?' He turned heavily in the bed and looked at her through eyes still half-closed with sleep.

'I don't know. I don't remember crying in the dream, I don't remember the dream, I don't think so. I'll get the tea.'

Rita put on her dressing gown and slippers and went downstairs. As she filled the kettle she saw her hand lifting a piece from the chess-board, about to make her move. The image was blurred, but she knew she was holding the queen. The White queen. She watched her hand fade from her visual memory and still she could see neither the board nor her pieces, just her hand.

What had she dreamt? She felt burdened and crushed by it and the fact that it was there as an indistinct presence and she could not remember it. Her eyes filled with tears: annoyed and puzzled at herself, she swiftly wiped them away and blew her nose as she heard her husband's heavy step on the stairs. He came in, a big, strong, gentle man whom she hoped she loved.

'Are you okay?'

'Yes.'

'It was very strange to hear you cry in your sleep. Racking sobs. Never heard you cry like that.'

He came close and took her in his arms.

'You sure you're all right?'

'Yes. I tell you, I can't remember what I was dreaming.'

She smiled at him as her eyes slid away from his, and hugged him before moving back to the stove.

'What time will you be back?'

'Latish, another damned meeting: I hate democracy. Listen, let's meet afterwards and have an evening out.'

Rita felt a moment of excitement, and immediately the image of the chess-board rose to her mind, Black aligned aggressively in a pyramid attack headed by a pawn, White inversely arranged in a futile attempt at defence. Before the image grew blurred again, she saw the White king apparently exposed on all sides.

'I've just remembered a bit of the dream. I was playing chess.'

'Chess? But you can't play chess can you?'

'I did.'

'You mean to say you can play chess?'

'I could.'

'How d'you do it? Married five years and still you manage to surprise me . . .'

Her husband's face looked rather foolish in his delight and Rita smiled at him.

'Still waters run deep.'

'They certainly do. Here I am, ex-champion of the local club, and it never occurred to me to ask if you could play. I just assumed you didn't.'

'I could have told you. I was quite good.'

'We must have a game. Who's got a chess set we know? I'll buy one today.'

'I don't want to play.'

'Why on earth not?'

'I don't know. I just don't want to.'

Her husband looked at her: Rita smiled.

'Hurry up or you'll be late. I'll get the post.'

Rita went to collect the paper and the post as her husband sat down to his breakfast.

She had been a tall, gawky and not very attractive eighteen-year-old when her parents had taken a house for the summer on the Adriatic coast. And there she and her brother had made friends with—what was his name?

As Rita cleared the table she hunted through her mind as if it was a drawer, casting aside and to the ground unwanted names, names that fitted different faces, names that had no face: she had lost it; perhaps if she did not look for it it would return to her—they had made friends with an elderly Englishman.

The memory of how they had met was gone, but the juxtaposition of a summer of meetings yielded a series of clear still-lifes. The hands were the most vivid detail: long, extremely thin and sometimes tremulous hands that hovered over the chessboard placed on a table under the pines, spotlighted by a strong ray through the pine-needles; the two of them at the centre of a magic circle where no sound could reach them.

After the first few games during which he had taught her the moves, they rarely spoke: his voice had been granular and warped by a lifetime of heavy smoking. He never smoked during the game. Occasionally, when she had made a good move she had anticipated with keen excitement, he would look up into her face and his grey eyes would smile behind the spectacles, and his mouth would twist into an invariably ironic grin.

They played every day. Every day, after lunch, during the afternoon siesta, in the stillness of the hot summer day highlighted by the hypnotic screeching of cicadas and the remote and almost unheard breaking of tiny waves on the sand, she would come to him under the pines.

To begin with they had played even four games in an afternoon, he checkmated her so easily; but gradually as her game improved the silence between them deepened, the hands moved more slowly, even the rasping of his breath would be unrecorded by her mind as she explored the possibilities in the next move, the opportunity for attacking or the means suitably to defend.

Rita walked upstairs to dress. Wasn't it strange that she could not remember the first time she had checkmated him? She would have thought that was the kind of event that would be indelibly printed in her mind. But she could not. She did remember—how could she forget—that winning had gained her access to his flat and to a special treat. What a child she had been at eighteen and how quickly she had grown after the end of that summer.

Winning did not become easier as she improved, it seemed to become more difficult. She could still sense the tension in every muscle, the tightness at the back of her head, the longing to win and accede to the treat that would be in store for her, and his ironic determination not to let her—he had obviously let her win at the beginning—and the mounting excitement the few times she had seen she could checkmate him whatever defence he brought to play.

'I wish I could remember his name,' Rita whispered as she cleansed her face, faintly shocked at herself for being able to forget it: his hands were so vividly clear in her mind, as if the sun had chosen to fix a constant ray to spotlight them all through that summer.

It had been Benjee's last summer, and what a summer it had been. The heat, the stillness, the deep gold of the days, of the sand, the piercing blue of the sky and sea, and Benjee's inscrutable eyes reflecting the sun, the black hair growing too long, matted by the salt sea. Rita let a dry sob rise in her chest as she remembered fully for the first time, her happiness, her excitement, her innocence, her drinking in of sun and sea; her parents receding into ghostly figures, barely seen or acknowledged during meals taken under the shade of pines. Incredible how full her empty days had been. Benjee and—and the old man. Rita cast her dressing gown aside and walked around the room as she put her pants on, then slipped the tights through long legs that were really too thin and shapeless, and a bra over breasts that needed no support. She walked up to the mirror and scrutinized herself as she often did. She was awkwardly put together: too tall, too spidery. Attractive mouth, yes, she could see that. And big eyes. But the shape of her face was all wrong. Too long. That summer she had felt beautiful; she had even put on weight on the strength of her feelings, and her olive skin had darkened and darkened and somehow had not peeled or scaled. She must stop thinking about it, why was she suddenly remembering it all? She had buried it deep, a jewelled casket locked in the grey safe of her semi-conscious mind. A golden casket, firmly closed, that should not be opened.

'Bloody dreams.' Rita thought viciously and pulled down the woollen dress over her head. Again the image of the chess-board, Black aligned in an attack, White cowering and retreating in a V-shape against the pyramid attack. Rita slid into her slippers and padded downstairs and into the drawing-room where she worked: she did freelance fashion design and invariably anticipated keenly her day's work.

She sat at the high stool facing the sloping desk and was immediately absorbed and remote from time and space and noise. Suddenly though the old man's hands superimposed themselves to the figurine emerging on the white sheet. Long thin hands, freckled with age, welts of purple veins standing out, the gestures deliberate and slow and inexplicably attractive in their age and knowledge.

She could hear the screech-screeching of cicadas, a slight murmuring breeze lifted the checkered cloth on the table, barely swayed the tall pines. The sun played through the needle-leafed green.

The old man's head was bent over the board, the glasses had slid down the arch of a thin-nostrilled nose, the hands now rested on the table. Then he lifted his right hand, hovered over the board and moved. He did not look up at her. He never looked at her when he moved, only when she made good moves, when his eyes smiled and his mouth grinned ironically.

Rita felt again the memory of the piercing disappointment when he had made moves that would prevent her from winning. She had wanted him to enjoy the treat as much as she did, had wanted him to cheat, but he never let her win after the first few games, and certainly the triumph and excitement were heightened to an incredible pitch the times she did. She would be trembling and shaking as he looked at her, smiling and ironic, and then rose from his seat and led the way into the flat after a victory.

Rita shook herself, felt a wave of nausea and rose from her seat. As she walked into the kitchen to make herself a cup of coffee, she thrust the memory of the man away. Surely there must be something she should be doing to get her out of the house? Why should she be suddenly dreaming of chess. She had not thought about it since it had all come to an end.

She switched her mind abruptly off as the kettle boiled, and made a cup of coffee. Consciously she turned her thoughts to the coming evening: Ian was very good at these surprise evenings out, she knew she would have a lovely time. A warm feeling of affection dispelled the nausea she had been feeling and Rita returned to her easel desk, lit a cigarette and looked down at her drawings. Some days she could do about a dozen drawings, and though eleven would be discarded, it usually meant that one would be full of promise. Other days her fingers seemed to slide awkwardly up and down the pencil, the lines would be equally awkward, the clothes faintly fantastic or frankly ridiculous.

As she looked at the unfinished second drawing of the morning, Rita knew that this was going to be a bad day. She knew, as she took a deep breath of smoke, that the pencil would burden her hand and scrawl aimlessly on the paper.

'Oh, no.' Nausea slipped back, and with it a name intruded in her mind like a clanging bell: 'Benjee.'

'No, I won't think about him.'

She rose from her stool and moved towards the phone. She would ring Ian. She was afraid of her thoughts and suddenly afraid of remembering her dream. She called through to her husband's office, but he wasn't there, and she left a message asking him to ring her. Speaking to someone had calmed her down and the nausea was dispelled again. Then the memory of the end of that summer was a flood in her mind.

Benjee had left a note to his parents saying that he loved them but that they would not understand so he had to go. They had called the police who pointed out that Benjee was of age and had clearly stated that he wanted to leave. And the English police had added that there was nothing they could do, as he had left from a foreign country, and they could hardly expect the Italian police to cooperate. Rita's father had made ineffectual attempts at hiring detectives to trace him, they had resorted to messages on the radio, ads in the papers, but they had never seen him again.

The golden summer had been dispelled like a diamond dew by the hard sun, yet Rita at the time had been almost ashamed and embarrassed at her lack of feelings at the loss of her brother. She had not really believed that he was gone and would never return: they had both run away so often as children. Her strongest feeling was one of resentment that he had not taken her with him as he had always done before.

After the two days of chaos and just before returning home, she had found time to slip away to say goodbye to the old man. But when she had reached the house where he lived he had not been waiting for her under the pines and when she had gone up the few flights of stairs to his flat and rung the bell, there had been silence on the other side, although Rita had had the uneasy feeling that someone had been there and was just not answering the door. She remembered looking up at his windows as she left, but they had been closed and shuttered.

They had returned home, and she had written to him apologizing for failing to turn up at their daily meetings and explaining what had happened, and giving her address in case he should return to England. He had not replied and now she could not even remember his name.

Rita rose from her seat near the telephone, determined to return to her easel desk and work, however much the pencil failed to obey her hand and her hand her brain. As she walked across the room the full vision of her dream returned to her: she had dreamt that she had won, she had moved the White queen and had won.

The old man's face was vivid from the dream, younger, the smile more ironic, the eyes steel-grey as he rose slowly from his seat and led the way into the house. She was following him into the sitting-room. The net curtain was being blown by a strong breeze. They walked, he ahead of her so that she could see his stooping shoulders and the creases of his trousers. They walked and walked through the sitting-room until they reached his bedroom where he paused and she stood still, facing him. He moved around her, and facing her back—she was looking straight at the window and here too the white curtains were dancing in a strong breeze—he reached for the collar of her blouse, ran his long fingers down her arm and removed it from the sleeve. She was back at the table under the pines, still playing. She was White and Black was mounting an attack. She had no chance of winning. It was his move.

Rita saw herself in the dream looking into the ugly face of her brother, whose hand hovered over the chess-board, made his move, then looked up. The old man's eyes smiled in her brother's childish face, the old man's ironic grin played on her brother's lips, but behind the old man's look were Benjee's inscrutable eyes.

They continued to look into the dreamer's eyes as Rita turned to answer the phone that had been ringing insistently. Her husband's voice did not diminish the clarity of the vision, but the gaze shifted to a middle distance beyond Rita's dreaming self, as if the dreamed presence was aware of the voice speaking to her, and by the time Rita had finished a brief reassuring conversation with her husband, the gaze of her brother's presence had warped into a cold look of knowledge and the recollection of the past was complete: though he had seemed to lose interest and had never participated in the daily meetings, it had in fact been Benjee who had first introduced her to Mr Honepure, the Englishman.

Mystery Story

Ghennema stood tiptoe on the stone tiles to rinse the glass, heard the crackle of an announcement and was at the station, pacing the platform overhung by a wrought-iron awning. She wore boots and a long charcoal-coloured fur, the hem of which left a light trail on the ground dusty with snow; the collar tickled her chin; her gloved hands, clasped at the wrists, were held inside a lilac muff and her hair tucked into a beret. She walked up and down between the bench next to a door marked Private and the exit, while the distorted voice insisted in calling out the unintelligible name of the place.

The awning was edged by ice stars and stalactites. Ghennema, still very thirsty, wondered whether her hands would get too cold if she were to break off a piece of ice to suck, removed the glove and stretched out a hand, looking around guiltily. As soon as she gripped the ice the crackling voice stopped: the silence was so deep it frightened her and she stuffed her hand back into the muff; and resumed walking, grateful for the crunching sound of her boots on the snow.

When the train finally arrived it hooted its way into the station from the opposite direction. Ghennema's apprehension was quickly followed by irritation when she tried to board it: the steps were high, she was not cutting a very elegant figure, despite the fetching fur and boots, by having to pull back the coat in order to place her foot adequately on the first step, and then having to heave herself up by gripping the metal bars on both sides. She had barely taken her foot off the platform when the train jolted forward with a screech. Ghennema clung to the bars, lost her beret, saw it roll under the big iron wheels, recovered her balance and stepped into the corridor as the train slid out of the station. The voice over the loudspeaker faded, the train gathered speed, the door slammed shut in a strong gust and there was only the beat of metal on metal and the hiss of the wind.

All the windows in the corridor were misted over. Ghennema walked down the carriages glancing into every empty compartment until she found hers. It was uncomfortably hot, but when she began to unbutton the fur she realized she was naked.—How silly—she thought: she had not been naked in the station, she had felt the folds of warm materials against her skin while she walked in the snow.—Naked except for a fur in an empty train going God only knows where—she thought.

It was all different this time: usually, in the middle of doing the most ordinary things—chopping vegetables, fixing a curler to her hair, peeing, washing her clothes—Ghennema would suddenly be at the station, waiting for the imminent train under the awning that protected her from the dirty drizzle which had been an inevitable part of the scene. Before she had time to get thoroughly chilled, the train would emerge from the east in a black cloud of steam. She boarded the nearest First Class compartment, sat facing the engine and looked out of a window that from being dark with dust and ash as they left the station, became ever clearer until the light was almost too bright, with the persistent glare of a midday sun. The train travelled west and Ghennema observed carefully what went on beyond. At times it went so fast the landscape was a mere blur out of which the look on someone's face would leap up at her and freeze against the glass. It crawled so slowly at other times, that she had leisure to see and take note of the scenes being played beyond her hearing but in clear sight. She had seen many things; men and women at work in fields, with babies on their backs or swinging in hammocks, riding on bicycles through villages or crowded cities, the children sitting astride the back wheels or perched on the handlebars, digging in back yards or sitting under the shade of trees in large gardens, walking and talking, always with children of every age, mothers and daughters linked arm-in-arm, fathers and sons gesticulating in silent argument; but only two scenes had recurred every time.

She had seen two children playing with a ball, throwing it against a wall and jumping and clapping their hands two or three times, or turning around on one leg before catching it. Each time the scene was slightly different: the ball was blue rather than red; one of the girls' white socks had slipped and gathered round the ankle so that Ghennema could almost feel the discomfort of material sliding further into the shoe and ruckling under the arch; their dresses were no longer the identical aquamarine blue they had been, but one might be green, the other orange; their hair too changed: sometimes it was short, sometimes dark, sometimes in plaits; and their features were usually plain unless they laughed when despite the metallic flash of braces, they were enchanting. One girl was always younger and plumper, and the wall against which the ball was thrown could be recently white-washed or with flaking pink paint; the house was in a clearing, an open field, an olive grove, perched against the side of a hill, next to a church. The train would steam on to the scene suddenly and seemed to pause for minutes before gathering speed. They had always played harmoniously except once, when Ghennema watched them in the courtyard of a farmhouse, and as the train slipped past she saw the older girl, viciously and without apparent reason push the younger child to the ground: the nearby chickens flapped their wings and Ghennema almost heard the hollow sound of head hitting concrete. Her heart gave a violent lurch, instinctively she rose from her seat with a cry and was back in the bathroom of her home, half-sitting on the toilet. She saw the girls in different contexts as well: with a group of boys wearing head-bands with feathers, carrying makeshift bows and arrows and jumping around in front of a tree to which the older one was loosely tied; walking together across fields where boys hid in ambush in the tall grass; the younger one lying on her stomach with a book in front of her, oblivious of the antics of the group playing what appeared like hide-and-seek. Although the scenes were accompanied merely by the regular thumping of the train, Ghennema could practically hear the sound of the children's yells.

Each time she had been on the train she had seen couples through the window of a tall rather dilapidated block of flats. The room was always the same: the window faced east, and the train, going west, came upon it at an angle that would have prevented her from seeing the whole room had there not been a large mirror on the northern wall. The mirror reflected the double bed against the southern wall, which was sometimes still neatly made up, and the man and woman sat on the end of it, facing the mirror, either holding hands, or kissing, or with his hand inside her blouse or lifting her skirt, or her hand on the zip of his trousers. Once the train had raced past without slowing down and Ghennema had caught a glimpse of a dark small man opening the door next to the bed to a handsome youth whose face she had seen reflected in the mirror; and once she had gone slowly past watching two women undressing each other, standing on the bed and laughing. Both scenes she had found distressing, so that when she was back washing the salad for the dinner party that evening, and buckling her sandals, tears had streamed down her face. Sometimes the couple—which was always different although she had seen the same man with a succession of women and one woman with various men—were already in bed and the scene was somehow less sordid and explicit. Usually she disliked the scenes because the glare of the sun made every detail of the room, of the bed, the imperfections of the bodies stand out too clearly and the atmosphere seemed painfully squalid. But there had been times, two or three perhaps, when something in the play of the sun on the train window, reflected by the half-open panes of the room and thrown on to the mirror to be cast upon the couple, had surrounded the love-making by a halo of light which had made her heart still, and when the train had steamed past she had experienced a sense of regret very close to mourning, that had remained with her even when she found herself back at the chores she had left behind to board the train.

This time it was different: when she turned to look out, the panes were frosted over and the landscape beyond invisible. Never before had she not been able to look out. As that thought crossed her mind, something went past outside the compartment. Ghennema dashed to the door and pulled it back: the passage was deserted, except for a black hat. It sat across the centre of the corridor, looking as if its owner had simply melted underneath it, and it was feeling guilty.—Napoleon's hat—she thought stepping close to it, and picked it up. She wanted to throw it out, it did not belong in the train, but her struggle to open the ventilation panels above the windows was unsuccessful. With a shrug to dismiss her unease, she

carried the hat back into the carriage, laid it on her lap and stretched her legs on to the opposite seat: the hat was a cat to the touch,
and she continued to stroke it mechanically for a while. Occasionally
she turned to the window, but though the frost was less thick and
she could see a little beyond it, the landscape remained shrouded
in a yellow fog through which the train cut, resolute but pointless:
the condensation curled and closed in on all sides.

Suddenly Ghennema was bored with a restive intensity that
resembled sexual anticipation. Uncertain which she was feeling, she
rose to her feet, letting the hat fall to the ground and trampling it
under foot—A cold bath, a brisk walk, think of something else, cool
it; must be the cat.—As she turned to go into the corridor her gaze
fell on the luggage rack opposite: there was something weighing it
down.

A book, a purple and mauve cloth-covered volume with a gash
of yellow lettering across it bearing the legend 'Mystery Story'.
—Another to add to the collection—Ghennema thought, peering
closely at the purples to distinguish the figures she knew would be
there: always a man with chiselled features and a woman with slim
ankles and short wavy hair, usually moving together but sometimes
separately, towards a house surrounded by threatening vegetation.
The silhouettes of the couple seen against the faint light from a
half-open door or french windows. But the gothic lettering hid any
figures.

Ghennema settled back in her seat, immediately oblivious, and
anticipating a good read opened the book. It was untitled, though
her name was embossed on the first leaf. Shaking with mirth she
turned the page and read the words: 'Pero credo la specie monaca
freshle turns to dew an ash.'—Nonsense—she thought, and flicked
through the blank pages until one towards the end which contained
the words 'Pero cant credan freshli speciel omana duet whore ass'.
Ghennema was immediately angry, flung the book across towards
the door of the compartment, saw a man peering in and became
aware that she had unconsciously unbuttoned her coat: the carriage
was stifling. Blushing she tried to cover herself, but seemed to have
acquired a lot of fat, the coat would not stretch across her breast
and hips, and even when she succeeded in buttoning it at the waist,
it opened above and below. The man raised his right hand: it was

folded into a fist except for the middle finger, which he wriggled at her, leering. Ghennema's eyes filled with tears as she tried in vain to pull the coat across and turned to the window, knowing he would come in. She heard the door being dragged back and felt the man's weight depressing the seat next to her. He stretched his hand and turned her face to him: there was no sign of a leer, just a warm smile and a slight smell of garlic when he bent over to kiss her. She smiled at him, feeling immediately pleased and comforted. He kissed her again and laid his hand gently where the fur fell open above the knee.

When she raised her head from the kiss, she glanced towards the door of the compartment with the thought half-formed in her mind that they should draw the curtains and saw the back of a figure, leaning with his head against the window, wearing the hat.

—My cat—Ghennema shouted, startling the man, and jumped up; but by the time she reached the door, the figure was no longer there: she gazed up and down the corridor, then marched from end to end of the carriage, walking sideways to have a better view of all compartments in case he was in one of them and slipped away.

—He's taken my cat—she explained to him when she got back.

—How do you know it was him?—he asked angrily, and strode off down the passage. She stared after him, her chest tightened into a knot that became a double knot when he turned around before reaching the door to the next carriage, leering again, with the middle finger wriggling upright in his fist. Then he raised his other hand and waved the book at her.

—My book—Ghennema yelled, running after him, and almost tripped over the hat, lying innocently across the corridor.

Sobbing she carried the hat back into the compartment and noticed something crumpled up in the corner of the luggage rack nearest the door. It was a black silk dress with tiny silver drop-shapes. Eagerly she drew the curtains, took off the fur and slipped into the dress. It was enormous: it hung loose almost to her ankles, and the sleeves seemed about twice the length of her arms. With great satisfaction she rolled them up, thinking:—nothing sexy here—and drew back the curtains.—All I need is a pair of specs—she thought, and laughed out loud just as a ray of sun penetrated through the deep fog, lit up the carriage and fell on the shabby seat, showing up the dust. Ghennema laid down the fur and sat on it.—Anyway, it was nonsense—she thought, missing the book.—And I have got the cat—she added, laying the hat carefully on the seat opposite.

—Now that's a funny thing—she said, talking to it—why you should be looking at me so quizzically.—She stared at it, then smiled.

—You're quite good company until the fog clears.—

—I'm going to sleep—she told it—don't let that devil come in.—

She patted the hat before tucking her legs under her, leaning her face on the side of the seat and shutting her eyes.—Wish I had a cigarette—she thought, forgetting she had given up smoking years before, and fell asleep.

She was woken almost immediately by the simultaneous glare of sunshine on her closed lids and the sound of the carriage door being pulled back: blinded by the light she could not see who had come in until a few seconds later, when a man had sat down opposite and donned the hat. He crossed his legs and looked at her: her heart began to pound, she turned to the window and to the familiar scene in the farmyard. The train slowed down almost to a standstill, and the children continued to dance in their game, one of them throwing the ball against the wall and catching it while the other, unable to keep still, turned handstands. Before the train gathered speed she had time to notice a woman, moving out of the shadows of the doorways where she had been watching the girls and taking some steps towards them. Then it hooted through a tunnel of foliage and Ghennema looked back to the man who had stretched out his legs on the seat opposite and was reading the book. The yellow title leapt at her.

—You can't read it. It's empty—she told him.

—No it's not—he replied, showing her the closely printed page he had been reading, Ghennema shrugged.

—You woke me up.—

—Yes. Welcome to the human race.—

—You're a devil—Ghennema said, restlessly unfolding her legs. He looked up from the book and grinned at her.

—You're no angel—he said. Her heart began to hammer against

her ribcage and she felt a blush spread through her face to her
neck. She rose to her feet and looked out at a group of children
running up a bank, followed by a man tugging at the hand of a
young child. Ghennema could see clearly the long untidy fringe
bouncing against his eyebrows and the look of impatience on the
adult's face. The man laid a hand on her waist.

—I want my cat back—she said.

—Of course—he answered, but did not remove the hat from his
head. Instead he got up and stood next to her. Both looked out of
the window: they were passing the city landscape she had often
seen before. Ghennema knew the train would slow down, knew they
would come upon another scene in the room: she didn't want to
see it, and buried her face in the man's chest. She felt one hand
stroking her hair and the other moving lower over her back as the
train slowed down with a hissing of brakes.

—Look—he said, raising her face and turning her head. The
window of the room was opposite: as if reflected in a mirror, she
saw herself, wearing the black silk dress, and the man, in the hat,
standing at the end of the bed, her arms around his waist, one of
his hands under her chin, the other stroking her back.

—Do you see?—he asked, breathing warm air close to her ear.

—I don't know—Ghennema replied, lifting her face to kiss him.
The book slipped off the seat as the train gathered speed and fell
at their feet, the garish yellow lettering uppermost.

Bachelor Life

July

Friday a.m.

Silence except for the ticking of the alarm clock. The bedroom is in
darkness though thin shafts of sunlight penetrate through cracks in
the curtains from a big east-facing window and alight on the thick
dark carpet. The door leading into a narrow passage and the rest
of the flat faces north. A dark walnut wardrobe is the only item of
furniture directly opposite the door and next to the window on the
south wall, the rest is aligned against the longer western wall. There
is a small double bed between a walnut chest with a bedside lamp,
and a chair. The white-washed walls are decorated with framed
prints and paintings, two big ones next to the door, one near the
wardrobe, one above the chest. The one above the bed is the only
one that can be seen in the twilight: it is a reproduction of Rublev's
Trinity in a heavy gilded frame. A man lies asleep on the bed, his
head half-buried under a pillow, his naked left arm clutching at
thick blonde hair. On the chair next to the bed, under an open
book, are his clothes. The trousers are neatly folded over the back
of the chair, on top of the jacket.

There is a second of a deeper, expectant silence before the alarm
goes off. The man rolls over, stretches out an arm, gropes for the
clock and switches it off. It is seven o'clock. He sits up in bed, with
his eyes still closed, and leans back against the wall. He yawns
largely, scratches his head, rubs his eyes and opens them. He rises
and, naked to the waist, leaves the bedroom for the bathroom where
noises can be heard: flushing of the toilet, water as the tap is turned
on, splashings as the basin fills, then the gentler sound of a razor
being frequently rinsed. He returns to the bedroom naked, takes
out a pair of pants from the top drawer of the chest and puts them

on. He goes to the chair and puts on the socks, held up by garters at the knee, the white shirt after checking that it is not badly soiled at the cuffs and collar, the trousers into which he stuffs the shirt-tails. He moves to the window and draws the curtains and looks out at the blue sky for a minute or two. He is tall, big-boned and fleshy, with surprisingly red, pouting lips and thick brows that overhang and cast shadows on the close-set blue eyes. He may be in his early forties, he may be as much as ten years younger. He turns and goes back to the bed, throws back the blankets and top sheet, rearranges and smooths the bottom sheet. He goes from side to side making sure the blankets are in place, the pillows are beaten into fluffi-ness, the bedspread hangs exactly on both sides. The alarm clock says quarter to eight. The man rewinds it, puts on the wrist-watch that had been lying next to it, and drops coins and keys into his trouser pockets, looks around to see that everything is tidy, then leaves the sunny room. He goes to the front door in his stockinged feet and downstairs to collect the paper, the post and the milk from the main entrance. He returns to the small spotless kitchen and prepares his breakfast. While the toast and the egg are cooking, he looks into the cupboard, the fridge and the vegetable rack, and draws up a list of shopping. He glances at a couple of bills, then settles down with the paper and the food, sitting on a stool at the work surface.

The man looks at his watch. Half-past eight. He folds the news-paper, gathers the dirty crockery and the saucepan from the stove and takes them to the sink. He leaves the breakfast things unwashed, though he wipes the work surface with a damp cloth. He returns to the bedroom, chooses a tie and puts it on, looking at himself in the mirror fitted to the inside of the left wardrobe door, above the tie rack. He rummages under the bed in search of his shoes, sits on the bed to tie the laces, then smooths the bedcovers and reaches for the jacket. He makes sure the wallet is in the inside right pocket by tapping with his left hand, checks the pockets of his trousers for keys and once more leaves the bedroom.

At exactly quarter to nine the man locks the door of his flat, carrying a briefcase and a raincoat. He walks down the steps, out of the building, turns right into a small back street, walks the length of it, crosses it and turns left into a main road. Some yards ahead is the Underground, and seven minutes after leaving his home the man is swallowed up in the morning rush-hour.

Friday p.m. The key turns in the lock at quarter past six. The flat is shadowy after a day of sunlight in the empty rooms. The man leaves his briefcase and a bulging carrier bag in the entrance and goes straight into a comfortably furnished sitting-room directly opposite the front door. He draws the dark-blue velvet curtains and moves over to a lamp next to a tray where there are some bottles. He switches on the dim light and fixes himself a drink. He sits on a large sofa, his feet on the small table in front of him, and lies back. Slowly, in the dim light and the silence he sips the drink in his left hand. His eyes are shut. Twenty minutes later he rises, pours himself another drink, walks down the narrow passage to the bathroom and turns on the hot water tap. The roar of water gushing into the bath accompanies him as he moves back into the passage, loosens and removes his tie, takes off the jacket, picks up the carrier bag and takes it into the kitchen. He unpacks all the tins and puts them in the cupboards above the work-top, leaves the jacket in the kitchen, returns to the bathroom and shuts the door.

His hair is wet and curly when he emerges, a towel around his waist. He goes into the bedroom and draws the curtains before switching on the light. He dresses with meticulous care in an elegant dark-blue suit, a tie to match, black well-polished shoes. Before putting on the single-breasted suit jacket he rubs his hair dry for a few minutes. He looks at himself in the full-length mirror fitted to the inside of the right door of the wardrobe, turning around, examining every fold and fall of the suit, brushing invisible specks from the shoulders and arms. At about quarter to eight the man is ready for the evening. He has tidied the bathroom, washed the morning crockery in the kitchen, fluffed up the cushion of the sofa where he had sat when he came in. He checks his trouser pockets for change, his breast pocket for the keys, switches off the light in the passage and leaves the flat.

Friday night. The key turns in the lock. The girl giggles as the couple is silhouetted against the light from the hall: she is leaning against him, and he is holding her by the waist. He kicks the door shut and they are plunged into the dark flat. The sound of the girl's giggles points to the direction they are going. They reach the bedroom, the girl bumps against something, gives a little scream and is heard falling on the bed. The man is silent and still for a minute, then he goes to the bathroom, switches on the light, quietly returns, shifts the girl, undresses her and puts her under the blankets. He returns to the bathroom, undresses, brushes his teeth, switches off the light and comes back to the bedroom. There is the densest silence throughout the night.

*

Saturday a.m. The man turns over, opens his eyes and sees the girl still asleep: her mascara makes a smudged shadow under her eyes, dried foundation scales her face in blotchy patches, her tousled hair is slightly greasy, her features in repose are no more than vaguely attractive. She is lying on her side facing the man with her cupped left hand next to her face. The man gets out of bed noiselessly and goes to the bathroom. The sound of water running wakes the girl who turns and looks around the room without recognition. When the man returns, fully clothed, the girl looks at him:

—I don't remember anything. I was drunk.—

—We were both rather drunk.—

He smiles at her, friendly. She smiles back.

*

Sunday a.m. The alarm clock goes off at six o'clock. The man turns over, switches it off, stretches luxuriously. He throws off the blankets, sits on the edge of the bed and again stretches himself. On the chair by the bed there is a rich-cream-coloured wrap. The man reaches over and puts it on. He walks into the bathroom, switches on the light and turns on the cold tap of the bath. He adds some liquid and turns the hot-water tap full on. The bubbles begin to form. He returns to the bedroom, reaches under the bed, draws out a suitcase, puts it on the bed, opens it and lays out a pair of women's pants, garters, stockings, a small-cup bra, a petticoat and a beautiful red woollen dress. In the bathroom the man looks at himself in the mirror: he lifts his left arm, puts the hand on the back of his neck and turns his head, smiling at his reflection: then he removes the wrap and steps into the bath.

The man is clothed in the woollen dress. He stands by the suitcase, opens it once more and removes a dark long-haired wig, a big jar of foundation, a stick of mascara, a compact with blue eye-shadow, a lipstick. He goes to the wardrobe and opens the left door: the tie rack is empty. The man fits the wig, careful to hide his own hair, and adjusts it to frame his face, looking at himself from all sides. He carefully lays the foundation more thickly on the chin and the cheeks to hide the dark shadow of beard, and adds the rest of the make-up, checking on himself constantly, backing away slightly to see the effect as each addition is made, grimacing and distorting his features as he brushes mascara on the upper and lower lashes. When the transformation is complete the man returns to the suitcase a third time, chooses a pair of black high-heeled sandals, a jacket and a black leather shoulder bag.

At quarter-past eight the man leaves the flat in his woman's clothes. He turns right into the back street and right again at the first junction. The high heels tick-tack down the deserted road, accompanied by bursts of birdsong. He crosses the road and walks swaying down yet another back street until he comes to a small church, grimy with soot. A number of early morning worshippers, mostly elderly women, are converging towards it and he smiles at them as they pass. He kneels in the second pew on the left, Our Lady's side, and buries his face in his hands. Throughout the service he stands, kneels and sits at the appropriate times, but does not join in the responses. During Communion he kneels, his face in his hands. At the end of Mass he remains kneeling as the church empties. When everyone has gone he rises and walks down the main aisle, smiling at the priest whom he meets coming up to clear the altar. The priest follows him with his eyes as he continues down the church and out.

November

Friday p.m.
At quarter-past six the key turns in the lock and the man enters the flat. His raincoat is dripping, his hair curled by the rain that can be heard relentlessly ticking against the glass. The man goes

into the sitting-room, draws the curtains, switches on the light and fixes himself a drink. He sits on the sofa, his head back, his eyes shut; a pause: the eyes open, the head lifts, the man takes another sip, lies back, shuts his eyes. Monotonous, metronome movements. When the drink is finished he fixes himself another, and then another.

It is well over an hour and a half later that he rises from the sofa with sudden urgency and swiftness, loosens his tie, walks into the bathroom and turns on the bath tap: then he walks into the bedroom, opens the wardrobe and starts removing clothes from hangers and throwing them on the bed. When the wardrobe is empty the man goes to the bathroom, turns off the tap and returns to the bedroom. He reaches under the bed for the large suitcase, opens it and begins hanging dresses, skirts and blouses where suits and trousers had been. The women's clothes are all beautifully tailored, obviously expensive items. When the clothes are hung and the underclothes piled in the shelves the man undresses, puts on the cream-coloured wrap, fills the suitcase with the men's clothes and returns it to its place under the bed before going back to the bathroom carrying a bottle. He pours some of the scent in the water and steps into the bath.

At nine o'clock the man leaves the flat dressed in an elegant salmon-pink dress, a neat black fur jacket, high-heeled boots and matching shoulder bag and wearing a carefully coiffed wig.

Saturday a.m.
It is completely dark in the bedroom and it isn't until the light is switched on that the man can be seen, wearing a wig of long brown hair and a lace nightdress. The alarm clock gives the time as nine o'clock.

In the bathroom the man removes the wig and the nightdress, fills the basin with water and shaves.

At ten-thirty the man leaves the flat, wearing a skirt and jumper. He swings a brown shoulder bag as he turns right and right again at the first junction. He crosses the road and turns into another back street. The sky is all cloud, and the leaves from the few trees litter the pavements. The streets are noisy with people engaged in

Saturday chores, but the insistent tick-tacking of the man's high-heeled boots seems the beat around which all sounds revolve until he reaches the church. Opposite there is a small ugly construction, and groups are queuing outside it: a big garish poster announces the Christmas bazaar. Proceeds will go to Cafod, the Catholic Fund for Overseas Development. The man joins the queue, smiling at those who turn and look at him until he sees them curl their lips and toss their heads.

Monday a.m.
The bedroom is in darkness, and rain can be heard pattering against the window pane. The man is asleep, his head half-buried under the pillow, his naked left arm following the shape of his head and hiding his features, his hand clutching at thick blond hair. On the chair, next to the bed, under an open book, are the clothes. Trousers are neatly folded over the back, on top of the jacket. It is just before seven.

February

Monday a.m.
At seven o'clock the alarm goes off, but the light is already on. The man lies in bed wearing a pink brushed nylon nightdress, his hands folded behind his head, pressing against the wig of long brown hair. He has been looking fixedly at the curtains. Wearily he switches off the alarm, removes his nightdress and wig and goes to the bathroom. As he shaves he stares at his reflection in the mirror. He returns to the bedroom and takes the suitcase from under the bed, opens it and picks out a suit. He looks at it and in sudden fury slams the case shut, sits on the bed and looks up: his eyes focus on the reproduction of the Trinity above the bed but the three figures look down with transcendent serenity, and the man falls on his knees and buries his head in his hands.

Communions

1

Her mouth is dry when she wakes up, and her heart is pounding. Violent sunshine streams through the open window, creates swords that pierce the air and light on the floor with the delicacy of warmth. Helen is aware of every sound: cicadas and birds still in competition at this early hour, the silence in the house clashing with the wakefulness of the countryside, a dog barking in the distance, another close by seems to bark in reply, a cock crows, sounds from the farm further up from the house fall loud and clear through the open window. Today she is making her first Communion: it means to eat the body of Jesus . . .

She stares at the light and the flowers and the sun-shaped object high above an altar ablaze with candles. The gold object is encrusted with jewels that reflect the lights; at its centre a round milky opaqueness contained in glass. It is the body of Jesus. The church is full and petals are strewn all the way down the main aisle; there is a strong scent of incense and lily. Around the altar-rail girls in white with long veils, boys in grey. The organ plays, the congregation sings loudly: Quemadmodum desiderat cervus ad fontes aquarum, ita desiderat anima mea dominum.

Helen is going to run away. She lies on her bed in the sultry afternoon and works it out. She will take her doll, her first communion dress, the book and she will run away. She won't tell anyone. She gets up knowing her mother and the baby are asleep, her father won't be back until late; the only person to worry about is Pina who is probably in the kitchen. Helen folds her first communion dress, wraps it in the cellophane envelope which had protected it as it hung in the wardrobe and remembers Pina's shopping bag. Quietly she opens the door of her room, slips past her parents' bedroom, tiptoes across the dining-room and the drawing-room, down the short passage to the back entrance. The large black bag is hanging from the hook: Helen steals it and returns to her room. There is no sound in the house, not even from downstairs in the kitchen. Pina must have gone out, and Helen remembers that if she runs away she must have food. She puts the bag under the bed and creeps out again, down the stairs off the dining-room. The kitchen is quiet and empty save for the hum of the refrigerator. Helen takes some bread, all the biscuits she can find, looks in the fridge and takes the smoked ham her mother bought for tomorrow evening's dinner party, and three apples. She wraps her booty in newspaper and runs up the stairs: but she drops the apples and watches them bounce noisily down like tennis balls. Though the house seems undisturbed by the clamour, Helen does not dare go and pick them up. She continues up to her room, where she packs the dress, the doll, the book and the food. At the last minute she takes the picture behind her bed: it was given her by her grandmother on her first communion day, and it shows the Sacred Heart. It is rather heavy, but small enough to fit in the handbag. She wonders whether to take her rosary, a present from Pina, but she doesn't. She takes instead a photo of her father, sun-tanned and smiling, taken down at the beach. She slips it between the covers of the book, zips up the bag, looks around to see if there is anything else she really would like to take, and then walks stealthily out on to the terrace, up the steps to the olive grove, past the olive trees and the vines. She is excited and elated, though the bag seems to get heavier with every step. As she walks Helen has the idea that the perfect plan would be to hide not in the beach house, but in the church: she can hide in the confessional, the priest does not hear confessions during the week. Once she has decided what she is going to do, she sits on the verge, takes out the doll and the biscuits and starts eating and talks to the doll.

The air is heavy and the silence extraordinarily deep. Helen lies back in the tall grass and watches some ants pushing the bigger crumbs from her biscuits. She falls asleep and wakes chilled to the bone; the bag reminds her that she has run away: she is very thirsty and wonders where she can find some water. The overcast afternoon has turned into a twilight without sunset and the silence waits for her to walk on. Helen begins to be apprehensive, picks up the bag in one hand and the doll in the other. She decides to make straight for her refuge: if she climbs the bank on the left of the path she will reach the main road, and from there she knows the way. As she clambers a few feet up, hugging the doll in one arm and dragging the bag in the other, and slithers down and clambers up again, the sound of pebbles and earth sliding to the path echoes loudly. She knows it will be easier to climb if she puts the doll back in the bag, but she is afraid and cannot bring herself to part with her and be alone, continues her slow climb through the stubble and reaches the top of the bank and the white dust road as the evening closes further into night. She is no longer cold, but she is so thirsty. She suddenly thinks of the tall marble water stoup that she can only reach on tip-toe: she can drink from there. She knows the way now, and the bag does not seem so heavy or the darkness so threatening. All the way there she thinks of the water, and how she will take one of the stacked chairs and put it next to the big, wide-rimmed shallow basin. Then she can scoop the water with her cupped hands and drink and drink.

She reaches the church just as the evening Mass is over, watches the few faithful disperse in the dark, enters the building and walks up the side aisle on her toes, until she reaches the confessional. There are a couple of figures kneeling in the shadow in front of the candle-lit statues of Our Lady and St Antony, and the rest is quiet emptiness. Helen wonders if she dare risk going to the holy water stoup at the back of the church, by the right-hand door. She looks at it with yearning, but the noise will attract the attention of the praying figures. She opens the shutters and slips into the priest's seat: she's never been this side, not even when they had that dare and Luigi tried to get everyone to go on the priest's side during Mass one day, and Helen's hands begin to sweat, wondering if she is committing a sin. She puts the bag on the ground and curls up on the cushioned seat, clutching the doll. She is very thirsty. She wipes her hands down her dress, sticks her thumb in her mouth and rocks, praying, please go, that she may drink. She remembers her mother hugging her then going to the baby, wonders whether she will be sorry if she dies and licks the tears as they reach the mouth; but they are salty.

She is startled by sudden movements in the church: footsteps echo in the silence, the door opens and crashes shut; Helen curls up into a tighter, smaller ball against the side of the cubicle. Another sudden movement, a bench is shunted forward and back, more footsteps, the door opens and closes. She is alone now, she can drink. Leaving the doll on the seat Helen opens the shutters and runs down to the entrance. She takes one of the chairs and carries it to where the stoup is, climbs and reaches for the water. There is only a very little in the basin and she dips her hand into it and puts it to her mouth to lick: it is lukewarm and salty. Helen slides from her standing position on the chair and sits; tears pour down her face and mingle with the undrinkable water on her fingers. Knocking her feet against the wooden legs, rocking with her back to the altar and her thumb in her mouth she sobs and sobs.

2

The Bishop murmurs unintelligible prayers, dips his thumb and forefinger in the oil and makes a cross on her forehead. Signorina Lena is behind her, and ties a white satin ribbon where the cross has been marked, to prevent the oil running down her face. Helen looks at the tall, powerfully built man: before he moves down the line to the next child, he stretches out his hand and, still murmuring prayers in Latin, pats her cheek with three cool dry fingers. Now she is a soldier ready to fight in Christ's army.

*

It is early. Light filters through the drawn curtains and the sound of waking birds penetrates the large half-open windows. The dormitory is quiet. Helen is awake, thinking. She thinks she is going to be a nun: she will wear a habit, be sent to the missions, perhaps become a martyr; perhaps die when she is twenty-eight, like St Thérèse of Lisieux; or be a doctor of the Church like St Teresa of Avila, Sister Demetrius' favourite saint. Helen thinks Sister Demetrius is a saint: she laughs, she says all saints laughed a lot. She has told her about the Carmelites: they walk around barefoot and never sit on chairs but on their feet. St Thérèse of Lisieux was a Carmelite. So was St Teresa. Carmelites have a brown habit, but they are not missionaries. The Sacred Heart nuns are. Sister Demetrius has told her that if she is very good maybe God will give her a vocation.

Helen starts to toss restlessly. She wants to get up, but the rules are strict, children must not leave their cubicles until the bell goes. If she gets up now and Sister Bartholomew sees her she will be reprimanded; but she cannot lie still any longer. She climbs down from the tall iron bed and puts on her dressing gown. Sister Bartholomew sleeps in the end cubicle next to the door; as Helen passes it she notices that the curtain is not completely drawn, there is a crack of about two inches through which she can see inside: the temptation is irresistible, she must look through. She goes near and peeps in. The nun, already clad in her habit, is kneeling by the side of the bed. A completely bald head is buried in the hands. Helen cannot move and the nun becomes aware of a gaze on her:

—What are you doing? Are you all right?—

Helen does not have the presence of mind to lie, stands there and looks at the head . . .

*

When the bell goes, Helen opens her eyes abruptly and looks at the tall ceiling above her cubicle: zig-zag cracks criss-cross it without pattern or reason. It's Sunday, the bell has been rung slightly later, and Helen lies smouldering until it goes a second time. Then she rises, draws the curtains and defiantly peels off her pyjamas in front of the window which gives on to a deserted patch of grass surrounded by beech trees in full bloom: it is raining thinly. Helen splashes water on her face and brushes her teeth, wanting someone to see her; but she dresses quickly into her Sunday uniform, a straight pinafore of indeterminate green. Knowing she should strip the bed, she doesn't, just throws the candlewick spread over it. She runs downstairs, down corridors to the refectory: she is late and doesn't give a damn, she thinks. The nun looks at her and Helen stares back, clatters in her chair as she sits down, though the noise is drowned in the loud chatter of the school. She is not going to talk to anyone, she decides; is quickly disappointed when no one addresses a word to her, and slouches back to her room to stand by the window waiting for the next bell, tense with irritation. The rain is so thin it is invisible, the beech trees and the grass glorify the day with their green, and Helen would gladly take the mug her father bought her when they went to Scotland and smash it against the window pane. She holds the object in her hand not really seeing it and thinks she is going to run away. The bell goes, but Helen stands by the window cradling the mug, refusing to yield to the habit of obedience. She decides to stay there until everything is silent, then pack a bag and leave, though where can she go? She does not have enough money to stay anywhere. She decides she'll become a whore, with a pimp. Or get picked up by someone in a car and become his mistress, in a flat with plants.

The curtain is pulled back and Helen's heart jerks. The nun speaks coldly and Helen puts down the mug and follows her down the passage, along corridors and into the church. The girls in her bench and the bench in front turn to look at her as she clambers into her place. At Communion Helen follows everyone else automatically to the rails. When the host is placed on her tongue, instead of swallowing it after carefully reducing it to pulp with saliva, she holds it on the tip of her tongue, returns to her place, buries her face in her hands and spits it on to her palm. She closes her fingers over it: the host retains some of the warm moisture from her mouth and by some trick of association feels as if it flutters for a second or two like an imprisoned butterfly. She doesn't dare open her hand, and stands with clenched fist to sing the last hymn. When she reaches the safety of her cubicle she opens her hand: the white wafer has stuck to her palm. Helen is filled with terror. She looks at the white disc clinging to her palm, glued to it by the moisture of her tongue, shuts and opens her hand hoping the flexion will release the host without damaging it; but the wafer is so thin it follows its contours and lines. She looks at it, afraid beyond reason to prise it off her palm, afraid to touch it with the fingers of her left hand, knowing it will certainly leave a burning red mark the size of a half-crown. She thinks she will go back to church and kneel and wet it, and perhaps it won't bleed if she is very careful. If she is seen she will be reprimanded, but she cannot touch the wafer until she is in church, she must risk it. Helen slips out of her cubicle and the dormitory; every board she walks on creaks, and her heart thunders painfully, but she reaches the relative safety of the passage where the toilets are. Now she must reach the chapel.

The corridor leading to it is deserted and Helen runs noisily, holding her fist clenched, until she reaches the door, goes in and kneels as near the door as possible, grateful for the permanent darkness, and prays that the host will come into her mouth without difficulty. As if in answer to the prayer, the wafer detaches itself from the palm as soon as her tongue touches it. Helen's throat is closed by a lump: it is some seconds before she can swallow it and as she does so tears of relief fill her eyes and spill over. She does not notice the quiet movement made by a nun who has been kneeling further up and is now coming down to the door. She lifts her eyes to a new apprehension as she comes towards her, but the old nun, unaware of the school routine, merely passes her with a smile of approval at her devotion.

3
—Come on, say it.—
—No.—
—Say fuck, fuck, fuck.—
—No.—
He is sitting on her belly with his hands pinning her out-stretched arms to the ground. she is half-laughing, unable to move; weakly and not seriously she tosses under him.
—I won't let go until you say it.—
—I won't.—
He bends over, kisses her fully, roughly on the mouth; at the same time he tightens his grip on her forearm.
—Don't, you're hurting me.—
—Say fuck me.—
—Please stop. I don't want to say it.—
—Yes you do. Come on, say it.—
—Please John, I've had enough. Let me go.—
—I want to fuck you. Say it.—
—But I don't want to. And I don't want to say it.—
Helen looks into his eyes; she smiles.
—Oh yes you do, you prim little bitch.—

*

Helen is wheeling the trolley around the supermarket: she has chosen vegetables, potatoes, onions, carrots, beetroot, cabbage, apples, tomatoes and is approaching the meat stalls. She thinks she'll have an abortion. One minute later, as she is picking up a carefully wrapped pound and a half of reasonably lean stewing steak, she is shocked at herself. Of course, she won't have an abortion, John will agree to support the baby, to help her. Perhaps she should marry him: she pictures herself married to him. No. She continues to select the shopping for the household and the word is an insistent beat; almost like a prayer, she thinks as she becomes aware of it and in the same breath prays, please God don't let it happen, let it go please. She doesn't want a baby. Perhaps she should marry him; and pictures herself married to him, the same picture of him kneeling over her, pinning her arms to the ground. She leans against the trolley and breathes deeply, feeling faint.

—Are you okay?—A woman speaks to her and Helen sees a large bust and lifts eyes to a kindly, fleshly, sagging face and brown eyes hidden behind thick lenses.

—You look terrible. I should get out of here if I were you.

—I'm all right, thanks.—

—No air in these places, that's the trouble. You sure you're all right?—

—Yes, thank you.—

The woman smiles and waddles away and Helen's sudden fury, the bastard the bastard the fucking bastard, dispels the faintness and she feels the colour returning to her cheeks. She chooses some cleaning items, Kleenex, toilet tissue, washing-up liquid, joins the queue at the till and her knees go weak with greed for the bar of dark plain chocolate she has not eaten since she was at school. She reaches for the biggest one on the rack, piles five more into the trolley and opens the sixth. When she has bitten into the hard thick slab she looks guiltily at the shoppers in front and behind her, sensing disapproval. Total indifference, eyes focused in the middle distance or unfocused in the blur of blank unthinking waiting restore Helen to a hesitant inner smile of irony . . .

At home she crouches on the threadbare carpet in the posture of primitive man, buttocks almost touching the ground, her knees level with her breasts. She swings on her haunches and concentrates all her thoughts on the first bar of chocolate. Then the second, third, fourth, fifth. The telephone rings but she does not pause: her mind has become a slab of dark sweetness, her body merely a swing. Incantatory words sing in her head; and later she kneels over the bowl and is so sick she hopes it won't survive, forgetting its safety in the womb, separate from all the entrails that contract again and again to eject chocolate, food, despair, water, bile.

On impulse Helen visits her school a week after. She takes the bus from the station to the village and walks the mile to the buildings made ugly by periodic additions of classrooms and sleeping quarters. The grounds though are beautiful: beeches, elms and plane trees contrast their varied green with the green of a grass speckled with daisies and buttercups, and gather, beyond the more open space around the building, into a thick cluster that rises above a tangle of low bushes.

Helen walks around thinking how, throughout the seven years she had been at the school she had never noticed its beauty, had never ventured into the fields or the wilderness. She is about to walk towards it when she hears the school bell and the automatic reaction of raised voices, laughter and chatter from the classroom. The chapel bell follows immediately, the familiar toll that had accompanied Helen's day-to-day school life, but the purpose of which she had never learnt or cared to learn. The sound fills her with panic, the muscles of her stomach tighten and she swirls around, determined to get the bus back to the station. Once she is at a safe distance, in the square of the village, she goes into the pub instead, feeling as she had felt the few times she had come as a gesture of defiance and rebellion when she was under age. She thinks, how ridiculous, orders a drink and some food and sits in the window seat looking out on to the square. While she eats, Helen remembers her former teacher, the agelessness of the strong-featured face, the stocky figure an occasional reminder of her humanity, as the shaven head of Sister Bartholomew had been a shocking reminder, and realizes why she has come: she wants to tell Sister Demetrius, she wants her help, she needs her help. Merely the thought of speaking the words fills her with relief; she'll tell her she should not have lost the baby, she should not have done it, she should not have aborted, of course she'll say that, but she won't be shocked, she won't despise her, she'll help. Helen imagines Sister Demetrius kneeling in the dark chapel, clasping he black thick-bead rosary, saying Hail Marys and thinking of Helen, willing all things well: all that matters is that she should think of her and the baby, that she should serenely and intensely wish her well. As long as she thinks of her just for a few minutes every day, then she'll be all right, then the baby will be all right even if she has aborted.

Helen finishes her bread and cheese and the drink knowing that speaking to the nun will somehow solve everything and feeling as if the knowledge that she will be speaking to her has in fact already resolved it. She feels happier and calmer than she has felt for the last few weeks and strides back in the early afternoon silence, past the village, along the main road to the gate, through the gate up the short, narrow, hawthorn-edged drive. The quiet is full of bird-song, the flapping of wings and the murmur of leaves. Helen walks eagerly to the front and rings the bell: a young nun she has never seen before opens the door and invites her in and through to the parlour, a shadowy room sparsely furnished with a table and wooden chairs. Helen asks to see Sister Demetrius, and when the young nun returns she tells her that Reverend Mother will be there in about twenty minutes, would she like to wait there or go for a walk in the grounds, it's such a lovely day isn't it? Helen thinks of the wilderness and what lies beyond it as she is accompanied to the door, but is told that the wood is part of the enclosure and visitors are asked not to go there. That's why she never went, Helen thinks; but she knows it is not: she never went because she had not the faintest curiosity about what was beyond the limits. Now it is too late. Helen sits on the dry grass under the tree, leans back and looks around, knowing she will not tell Sister Demetrius after all: the unknown nun called her Reverend Mother; or she called the Superior because Sister Demetrius is no longer there. Helen does not want to talk to anyone else, or even her if she is Reverend Mother now. There is no point in waiting, she won't tell her, too much has changed. She may be dead. Why else call Reverend Mother? She doesn't want to know.

Helen rises and walks away, feeling she has lost something of incalculable value; half-hoping to hear the sound of the door opening and the familiar voice of Sister Demetrius calling her back. She is about to enter the main road when she turns and thinks she sees a black-clad figure emerge from the doorway, but she is too far away to see who it might be and doesn't stop.

Phebican

There was a girl who was born in a land of flowing rivers and tall trees. When she was tiny her mother rocked her to sleep against her breast and when a little older her father carried her on his shoulders, holding her legs; her feet knocked against his chest and she wrapped her hands around his forehead. Older still, she wore pigtails, ran and skipped all day in and out through the tall trees and slept at night to the murmur of the flowing rivers.

She had brothers, sisters and friends: girls with brown and black eyes who did not wear pigtails but fringes, boys with buck teeth, large ears whose lobes they could move, lips that pursed in melodic whistle, grubby hands and grazed knees. They chased each other in and out of the sunlight, swapped sweets and toys, cried and laughed. In the evening she was the first to be ready and sat in her father's lap to hear about the princess who felt a pea under one hundred mattresses.

Her name was Penelope Helen Eve Beatrice I Circe Albertine Nausicaa, but she had many nicknames formed by the initial letter of each name: Phenacib, Phibacen, Chipaben, Chebinpa, Banchepi, Bicanphe, Benphaci and her favourite, Phebican. The year her mother began to plait her hair Chebinpa wondered whether the 'I'— hardly a name— was just to make it easier to find nicknames for her. She experimented with the seven initials, came up with four ugly-sounding words, Chenbap, Chenpab, Phenbac, and for a while demanded to be called Phebanc; but she soon forgot.

One morning when her hair was still in plaits, Phebican woke up with a weight pressing down on her chest: it was a leaden sphere about one foot in diameter, attached to an intricate chrome chain more than five feet long, that remained taut and vertical as if held by some invisible pulley in the ceiling. It must have weighed at least ten pounds, and Banchepi was quite suffocated by it. She tried to wriggle away, but it rolled with her as she moved to the left in the empty space of her parents' big double bed, and when she rolled on to her stomach it pressed between her shoulder-blades, pushing her ribs into the mattress. Breathing was even more difficult, and she turned over on her back again, taking quick shallow breaths. The weight lifted slightly when she moved, but as soon as she lay still it settled into her chest again.

For a while Phebican tossed back and forth, thinking it would go away. She lay on her left side, then on her right, then on her stomach, returned to her back and began to turn again: when she was on her side the sphere dug into her arm and blocked the flow of blood. She could breathe more easily, but the numbness after the pins and needles soon forced her to change position.

For a further while Chipaben lay still on her back, letting the weight sink in, hoping the sphere would go away, not breathing except in spasms. To distract her she observed the chain: it was beautifully detailed, the chrome shone like white gold— perhaps it was white gold— and the links were delicate petals and strong stems of differently shaped flowers, stem joined to petal, petal linked to petal, petal joined to stem. Phebican turned on her side to breathe more deeply, then returned on her back: each link was about three inches long, the flowers were small and distinctive, and although absolutely flower-like, they looked like no flower she had ever seen. She turned on to her left side, breathed deeply, turned on her back and squinted at the sphere crushing her chest into the mattress. Unlike the chain, it was dull and opaque, absorbing all the light that poured in through the window directly facing the bed, and creating an area of shadow over Bicanphe's face and neck.

Lying on her side she could see the cloudless, intensely blue sky. The tops of the tall trees swayed at the touch of a warm breeze, and the distant sound of cicadas had already overtaken the morning call of birds. Benphaci wanted to open the window completely and let the summer morning air flood in. She rolled to the edge of the bed; the sphere lifted above her as she tried to sit with her legs over the side, and shifted on to her shoulders so that she had to stoop. When she rose to her feet it moved and rested on top of her head.

By the time she reached the window, Phebican's neck was taut and stiff from bearing the weight, and her head felt flattened and bruised. At least she was no longer stifled. She breathed the clean country air and looked out at the beloved landscape for a while, but the weight almost closed her eyes in pain and she had to move again to try and dislodge it. She walked back to the bed and the sphere rested lightly, merely brushing the top of her head as she moved. She stood still and it was as if the pulley let the chain down one more link and the sphere rested all its weight on her. Chebinpa shook her head violently, ducked lower, knelt on the floor, lay on the floor praying that the chain would not be long enough, but after a few seconds of respite the weight was on her head and then her back once more.

Phebican got used to it and found devious ways of escaping it for stretches at a time. The secret was to keep moving, though the faster she moved, the sooner the weight settled again either on her chest or on top of her head or on her shoulders. She developed a slow rather jerky walk, a restless and constant movement that ensured the weight only brushed her during the day. At night she slept at irregular intervals on her side, and in the morning it took her some minutes of flexing and massaging to get the circulation going again in her arms. For as long as she could bear it she would lie on her back and look at the chain: there must be flowers like the flowers of the chain and she demanded to be taken to greenhouses, nurseries and for long country walks in search of them. One day her mother suggested she should have her hair cut and curled, and Phibacen emerged from the hairdresser without the leaden weight dogging her every step. It had gone.

The sphere had stunted her growth and Phebican grew several inches in a few weeks, put on weight because she could sit through a meal without having to move around all the time, lost the haunted look of those who sleep little and the grey pallor that had covered her face was soon replaced by the rightful glow of youth. In time she forgot the sphere, but the memory of the chain determined her career as a botanist. She specialized in archaeological botany and travelled extensively in search of fossilized flowers and ancient seeds that could be coaxed into life by the right environment. She shed her nicknames and was called now by one, now by another of her names.

One year Penelope went to examine a unique flower that seemed, in its minuteness, in its elegance, to defy the loud blowsiness of all other flora in that tropical area. It was an exquisite creation that could not be transplanted: the various experiments that had been made to try and grow it in greenhouses had only floundered and endangered the rare species. There were speculations about its similarity to flowers that grew in totally different environments, and arguments as to its origin and its place in the scale of flower evolution. She had gone to analyse and compare it and its seed with specimens she had accumulated in her world-wide research.

During her stay, one day of intense heat and humidity, as Helen walked through the tightly packed undergrowth towards the secluded area that sheltered the flower, she felt the forgotten but familiar pressure at the top of her head. Soon the muscles of her neck were painfully strained from bearing the weight, and she had to sit down. After a short while, to relieve her head, she lay on the steaming foliage of the forest floor. The weight lifted slightly and shifted to her chest: the chain was much longer than it had been before, stretching up as far as she could see. The sphere itself was about double the size it had been and weighed at least two stone. I was forced to lie on her side to breathe and to turn from one side to the other. There was no question of her being able to breathe at all if she lay on her back: the air was too thick with humidity for the short shallow breaths the weight allowed. She would not be able to reach the flowers with it resting on her head; she rose to her feet trying to remember the jerky walk she had acquired in the past to minimize the weight and by the time she reached her lodgings she felt confident enough in her walk to think it was the most ludicrous thing that had ever happened to her and to decide to ignore it.

It was difficult to ignore. Eve reacquired the mannerisms she had developed as a child to escape and to cope with the weight, but it soon became clear that she would have to leave the country: breathing was almost impossible in the thick atmosphere. She had not been able to lie on her back for long enough to see the chain in any detail, though she saw that it was made not of chrome, but of platinum. As soon as she returned to the land of flowing rivers and tall trees and to the fresh dry air she lay and looked at its intricate beauty. The flowers looked like no flowers she could think of: not speedwells, not daisies, not forget-me-nots, not wild cyclamen, certainly not roses or camellias or orchids, not even the rare tropical species she had been studying, yet as she looked, breathlessly weighted down by the sphere, all these came to her mind.

The careful, painstaking observation of the archaeological botanist had required hours of immobility that became impossible with the sphere crushing her. Beatrice was forced to leave her work and took on a job as gardener in a large estate. She had constantly to stoop and straighten to dig out weeds, and the sphere bounced gently up and down, barely brushing the top of her head or her shoulders. Even so, her body was soon twisted in an unnatural way— the left shoulder so much higher than the right it resembled a hump— from the effort to escape the weight. The tropical tan disappeared and Beatrice's face reflected the dull grey of the leaden sphere. Once again, after restless cat-naps disturbed by the need to toss and turn, I would lie on her back for as long as her breath held and contemplate the luminous chain stretching to the ceiling: it was as if it had taken every ray and speck of light, transformed it into something purer and then cast it out into the room. The only area of shadow remained over her face.

One day in the garden Circe met a man with blue eyes: the pupils were big and black like a child's, and at times the intense blue was a mere halo around the black. They played together, but the sphere impeded her movements, made her clumsy and ungainly, and the day came when he lifted it from her and Albertine watched the taut chain slacken as he carried it to a corner of the greenhouse. When they looked in that direction again a long time later, the weight was no longer there, though the corner was littered by a small pile of lead shavings. Before too long they tired of their game, the man walked away and Nausicaa continued to work in the garden, digging out weeds, planting flowers and shrubs, mowing the large lawn, scything where the lawn-mower couldn't reach, underneath the tall wide-branched trees, lying by the river when her work was done, until she had saved enough to buy a reasonable quantity of platinum.

I moved to a little hut close to the river and spent a long time trying to remember, by drawing them, what the flowers of the chain had been like. Sometimes a fraction of the lower part of one particular petal I had just drawn would remind her quite strongly of one flower, but when I cut it up and joined it to another portion of the same flower she had pinned up on the wall of the hut, both parts lost all resemblance to the original. At first I threw the failed attempts away, tore them up and burnt them in the fire-place she had built in the centre of the room to keep herself warm during the brief winter months; but as she began to be reminded of the originals in the fragments, I began to keep them all, and pinned them around until the whole hut was covered with drawings of parts of flowers and stems. Finally, knowing her time was running out, I began to build the mould for the platinum chain: it was to be just three links, and imperfect as it would undoubtedly be, I wanted to make it. On the morning she was going to melt the platinum to pour into the mould, I woke to the familiar pressure: the weight was even greater, even heavier. So heavy I could not move. When she tried, the sphere did not lift obligingly as it had done, but pressed into her relentlessly. Above its leaden, suffocating weight, I could see the delicate radiant chain, stretching to the ceiling, more beautiful, more intricately fashioned that I had remembered. As the weight shallowed the breath into gasps I turned her gaze around the hut, looked at the sketches, recognized the hopeless inadequacy of her drawings, rejoiced that she had not fashioned anything in durable platinum, shut her eyes, and opened her mouth in one last attempt to breathe. The shadow covered her face and the sphere crushed her body.

The Fire Eater

Today's description by a friend of a household in Rome— an American woman with two girl children and a man friend who is a fire-eater: a door springs open in my brain, the thought shoots out like a cuckoo from a clock, 'story possibility, story possibility'.

The name—Barbara Grimes.

They are there, in the back of my head, titles, names, an episode, an action, a gesture—and here I am, torn between writing and making a cup of tea, between the physical activities of picking up a pen and drawing the curtains against the oncoming night. At this moment the pen is winning, but the war is not won. Soon it will be time for me to change, to leave, to go out for an empty evening and this pen will be put aside with a sigh of relief overlying a strange melancholy, as of an opportunity lost. And tomorrow the effort of lifting the pen, of writing—no, not even of writing but of thinking through what I want to write—may be too much and the pen will lie quiet, the paper fallow. But I must have a cup of tea.

I am back, armed with tea and cigarettes. I have an hour. What man is a fire-eating man? Piecing together from images the picture. There is a story in that group: the man poised with the fire, about to swallow flame; the woman impatient, American, extrovert. The children, shadowy elves constantly changing, like all children, still cell-like beings assimilating the outside. There is a story. There is a story in Barbara Grimes. She wears glasses, she is small, squat, ugly, middle-aged. The spinster. I classify because I want to shape, I want Barbara to meet the fire-eater. Shall she fall in love? With a fire-eater? There, the germ of a story, fire-eater meets spinster.

Why all this effort though? Why bother to write at all? Is it every possible me or is it the all-mysterious other I want to understand? Is it revelation I want or mere description? Is it story-telling or metaphor? Or is it indeed all these things? And why as I wrote, just as I wrote, did Barbara Grimes and the fire-eater come together? I had no idea, writing the first page, that on the second page the man poised with fire in his hand, gathering a crowd of tourists and children in Piazza Navona, was going to be connected with the spinster. She must come on holiday. Or shall she come as a nanny? But then, the American woman is not rich, no, her flat is too small, Barbara would have nowhere to stay. And anyway, she has no experience of children (I cannot picture her life before this moment. Is it important? Does one need the illusion of a before and after to make sense of the here and now?)

Why write? Communication? Perhaps, but that does not explain the desire for fiction, and though I admire writers who transcend fiction in an effort to reach some kind of centre to the experience of being, my mind floats up from such depths to the surface of story-telling. Is it not therefore, another, not myself, that I seek? And yet—I am not interested in people. I am not interested in people. I am not interested in Barbara Grimes, or the fire-eater: were I to meet the actual acquaintances of my friend who correspond to these labels, I would be, at best, indifferent. At worst, disappointed that they bear no resemblance to the figures in my head. It is the name, and the action to which something inside me responds. There is some kind of mystery in that name and that action, and I want them together to see how they react to each other. Like electricity, the joining of neutral and live in a mere hair of copper—do you know how it works? Putting on a plug is an eternal mystery for me. But perhaps it is simpler than I am prepared to admit.

The hour is up. I was beginning to enjoy myself.

Barbara was hot. It was stifling on the plane, a rickety DC10 whose air-conditioning system seemed to have failed. She wondered passively if all the passengers would die from lack of air before they reached Ciampino. But no one seemed to notice the heat. Barbara took off her thick-rimmed glasses and rested her head back. The novel which she had picked up because the name of the author was the same as hers, and was not enjoying, lay open on her ample lap: the subdued print highlighted the flowery print on her cotton skirt.

She reached out for a cream-coloured handbag, took out a handkerchief and mopped a square, mannish face, softened by rather beautiful brown eyes soon hidden behind the glasses.

Shall I describe the landing, the transport into Rome, the finding of the *pensione* Barbara had carefully booked from Dunmow in Essex, the trickling shower she managed to take to cool off, the careful unpacking of her case, the displaying of the treasures she had to bring with her, a fading photograph of her parents on their wedding day; another of her mother the year she had died, a stone which had been given to her about thirty years before by one of her teachers on whom she had had a painful and anguishing crush; a shell she had found on the Norfolk coast one autumn day, which shone with a delicate pearly light; a much leafed-through Bible (Revised Standard Version)? Shall I describe the lonely wonderings of this middle-aged spinster among the rich beauties of Roman churches, the awe at the eternal magic of the Eternal City? Or shall I dwell on the crushing heat of the July days, the burning pavements, the high-pitched squeal and then the continuous scream of the tourist whose bag had been snatched by black-haired youths on scooters (Barbara quickly changed her bag to the hand on the pavement side); the loveliness of the cooler evenings, the cafés crowded with tourists and Italian families, children rushing around the piazza engaged in some game whose rules were unfathomed by the adults sitting drinking and talking? No, let me leave her to the privacy of her holiday abroad until the evening she comes to Piazza Navona. Shall it be a week after I have introduced her to you, and to myself, waiting on the plane? Is action the essence of story? Is it the events or her feelings that concern me and you?

This is the third time I've mentioned you. Who are you? The perfect reader, faceless, sitting in a leather armchair in a pool of light from a standard lamp, surrounded by darkness, as if on a stage; turning the pages, always turning the pages. Do the fire-eater and Barbara interest me because through them the ghostly reader will remain still in his chair and turn pages of the thick heavily bound book on his knees? Do I write from love of that power over you that keeps you reading? And how can I ask you, who, if this is the reason, are a puppet whose hand I lift with my string of words? I should keep it to myself and just give you the story: you're much more in my power if I do.

Barbara had been to Piazza Navona during the day some days before, but that evening she was drawn to it again. She had returned to the hotel after a gruelling day sight-seeing, and lay on the sagging mattress for a while, too tired to move even to the shower she knew would refresh her, staring at a crack in the ceiling no effort of the imagination could transform into anything. The shadows lengthened, and her mental restlessness increased as physical exhaustion was beginning to envelop her in a wad of torpor. The picture of Piazza Navona rose to her mind with insistence, as of a refuge from the barrenness of the room and the intrusion of the cracked ceiling. When its persistence became compelling Barbara rose, shuffled to the shower, stood under it for some minutes without moving, not washing but letting the water cleanse her and wake her. She slipped on the slightly soiled dress she had been wearing all day, rubbed her short hair with a towel, put on the flat comfortable shoes she had been careful to buy in Dunmow, picked up the cream-coloured bag, checked that she had money, hunted around for the key to her room and finally left it—

I have not described all she did in the three-quarters of an hour between rising from the bed and leaving the room: if I were to examine what she does from the moment she gets up to the moment she goes to bed it might make a brilliant list of activities, but it would certainly be unreadably dull. Too real, and we do not like reality, we create the world that surrounds us, we do not look at it. The reality of Barbara is dull. I would like to transform her, make her into a Beatrice—or even just a woman whose beauty is the purpose of her life; or an ugly woman who has some purpose in life, even if it is an alien one, being a collector of fish, or matchboxes. Barbara does not collect anything. Not even memories. She has forgotten her parents, except for the mental picture which is an exact reproduction of the wedding photo on her bedside table. She has forgotten the unbearable love of her teens, though she has never loved again; and the Bible is a habit: she reads it, unfailingly, every night before sleeping and every morning before rising, but without making it into anything, as one reads advertisements from tube trains. The shell is the only real thing.

I would like to make her into fiction. Tomorrow I will sit at my desk and write of a Barbara who is and does all that Miss Grimes cannot because of what I have made her by the words I have used, the surname I have given her. I can, of course, tear these pages and throw the middle-aged spinster and the fire-eater into the waste-paper basket. If I do not like her reality, why don't I do that? Because, if I am writing at this moment to avoid the meeting between Barbara and the fire-eater (I don't really know what will happen), I still want to know what happens; though the man, apart from the gesture of eating fire, is nothing: he has no name and I cannot think of one. That he has a mistress—I was surprised, somehow a fire-eater hardly seems human and in need of love and sex—and that his mistress should be American and with two children, that enfleshes him in part. He is, of course, Italian. Why of course I don't know, but he is. Is he kind or brutal? Will he love Barbara or use her, or both? Or will he be completely untroubled? Or will he not know? Will Barbara's love be a repetition of the adolescent love, an unspoken if obvious passion which will never be consummated? Yes, I think that will be it. And to him she will be just what she is, a rather pathetic spinster whom he talks to by accident (I think he will singe her hair), and whom he will perhaps invite once or twice to have a drink from some never-analysed sympathy.

I am telling you the story before it happens. We have left Barbara shutting the door on her bare room and the cracked ceiling, descending the cool stone steps, entering the outside world with a sigh of relief—

Now we know what happens, can I wield enough power to keep you turning the pages if I keep talking instead of getting on with the story? Or will you shut the book, impatient of the chatter that comes between you and it? Ah, but if you close the book, in the darkness I can go on, despite you. If I seek anything, it is power to create and alter events, not power over you, to keep you reading. What use is a further puppet, watching puppets who obey my bidding at the writing of a word? You are only an appendage, I don't write for you but for myself. I don't write to communicate but to explore, I don't write to reveal but to discover; the light is for me to see by, and the mystery is not in the combination Barbara Grimes–fire-eater: words are the live hairs of copper along which the power travels. The spinster and the Italian man (I'll give him a stereotype, irrelevant moustache) are the neutral I need merely that they should combine with my words to generate light. I give them existence not for themselves, not for you, but for the sake of the light; and they need me to exist, but neither they nor I needs you for them to exist, so you can shut the book. I don't need you. I just need Barbara Grimes, stuck on the last step of the stone staircase, about to breathe her sigh of relief, about to go forward to meet her last love, about to suffer when I write the word pain, to laugh as I write to laugh, to gaze with the rediscovered wonder of childhood at the phenomenon of someone appearing to swallow and eject fire. There, she is outside now, I have put her outside with my word. She is walking slowly past the penumbra of the narrow streets where her hotel is, into the wider roads punctuated by the light from the shop windows, moving inevitably with my pen towards the man. And now I can just say that she has arrived and the walking is no longer necessary. She is there, sitting in this café, surrounded by undefined figures who, if I should focus with my pen, would be transformed into men and women with lives, but whom I am content to label people and tourists.

Barbara noticed a knot of people at the opposite end of Piazza Navona, but she could not see what was happening. Occasionally faces would be silhouetted by a bright light which quickly faded, and laughter and clapping would follow. People joined the group and detached themselves, and Barbara became aware of the silence. Adults were still talking at tables all around her, but the high-pitched squealing of the children's games no longer formed the background. Her curiosity increased, she paid for her *granita* and moved across the piazza, clutching the bag in permanent fear of the *scippatori* who sprang from nowhere. All the children were there, and as she came near, through a gap in the crowd she saw a flame come out of the mouth of a small man and quickly vanish. Laughter followed, the man bowed to his audience as they clapped, coins hit the ground all around him and a blond urchin who had been standing next to the man rushed around and collected them, grinning from ear to ear. As Barbara joined the fringe of the group the man put the lighted torch to his mouth and again a flame sprang up out of it, lit his face and then faded. The ritual of bowing and clapping followed and then the man said: 'Signori e Signore, un'ultima volta.' Curious to know how it was done, Barbara pushed to the front as a sigh of disappointment passed through the crowd. The man moved slowly, walked around in a circle with his arm extended, the hand holding the torch towards the crowd, waiting for the right pitch of suspense, for the moment when the children's eyes were glassy in anticipation, when the murmuring had stopped and all eyes were on him. He returned to the centre of the circle, and with his back to Barbara thrust the torch into his mouth. The flame was greater than before, and seemed to last longer: a few seconds of the deepest silence except for the exhalation of the man's breath—and then the release into laughter and clapping. The man, suddenly small again, barely taller than the tallest child present, bowed and smiled and told them he would be there again the next night, thanked them for their generosity, winked at a tall girl, pinched the cheeks of a child whose eyes had not yet lost the glaze of wonder, waved at everyone, bowed again as his urchin mate finished gathering coins and dropping them into a pouch, thanked them again and as he backed out of the circle bumped into Barbara.

—Scusi, signora, mi scusi, mi scusi.—

The apologies flowed profusely, and his eyes smiled almost more than his lips when Barbara said in broken Italian that was all right, it was her fault, she could have got out of his way. She fumbled in her bag and took out a note.

—Grazie, signora, grazie mille. Buona notte, buona notte, grazie.—

Still backing the small man bowed and thanked, then turned and walked quickly away, his retinue following at a trot. As the crowd dispersed, Barbara saw the charred remains of the torch, absentmindedly picked it up and, slowly walking across the piazza, returned to the shadowy street where her hotel was and into her room. She placed what was left of the torch on the table, removed her clothing, put on a pair of pyjamas, brushed her teeth, slipped under the sheet and put out the light. The crack was still visible on the ceiling, lit by the light darkness of the summer night. After some time Barbara switched on the light again, reached for her Bible and began to read it.

The next day Barbara was there early. The crowd had not yet gathered in the cafés around Piazza Navona and the waiters were lounging at the tables, drinking coffee in preparation for the evening ahead. Barbara sat at the same table she had sat at before and gazed at the empty piazza. She sipped her drink slowly, but time had not moved when she had finished, except for a deepening shadow and the lighting of a few more windows in the houses that circled the square. There was a small trattoria at one end and Barbara, who had put on a billowing wide-skirted dress that made her appear stouter than she was, walked to it and sat down at a small table outside. She ordered food she knew would take some time to be ready and sat back, her eyes fixed still on the piazza which she could see through the tall potted plants that formed a hedge around the restaurant. It was Rome's quietest hour; the noise of traffic was muffled and far away, the inhabitants of the city were mostly at home having their evening meal, the tourists were resting after their day of discovery before re-emerging to experience Rome by night.

The trattoria had been practically empty when Barbara sat down, but gradually as her first course arrived and was consumed and was followed by meat and then fruit, the tables were filled, the silence was replaced by the hubbub of chatter and laughter, and the evening had begun. Barbara returned to her position at the café and ordered another coffee-ice. Although she felt she had not taken her eyes off the piazza, she missed the arrival of the fire-eater. He was suddenly there, surrounded already by a small crowd, invisible but perceived by the faint light that emphasized the silhouette of the people around him. Barbara walked quickly across and joined the fringe of the group. For three-quarters of an hour the man repeated his magic every five minutes or so. People came and went, the urchin, whom Barbara now saw was a girl, collected the coins that clattered to the ground, the man bowed and thanked. Barbara stood first at the edge, then at the front of the crowd, joining in the clapping and the laughter each time the act was repeated. Then the words:

—Signori e signore, un'ultima volta—and the ritual ceased. Barbara pushed her way around so that she was facing the man, and as he bowed and thanked one last time, she handed him another note.

—Grazie, signora, grazie—oh, buona sera signora. Le piace allora il mio gioco?—

Barbara nodded.

—È Inglese? I spik Inglish, yes a leetle inglish, yes.—

—Very good English.—   .

Barbara nodded and smiled.

—No, not verry goodd, mai pronanzation not goodd.—

The child tugged at his sleeve and then turned to Barbara and said in English with a strong American accent:

—Hi. He is hungry, he must eat.—

—Are you not Italian then?—

—No, I am American. We must go. Goodbye. Dai, vieni, andiamo.—

—Goodbye.—

—Gooddbai, tenk you.—

The man smiled at her with his eyes and walked quickly away, leaving another charred stump which Barbara picked up.

The following evening Barbara invited the man and the child to have something to eat. They agreed eagerly and Barbara watched them as they devoured a large meal with the concentration of real hunger. The child then chattered in English, the man nodded and smiled, agreeing with what she was saying, obviously not understanding most of it. Barbara learnt that the child had a mother and a sister and that they all lived in—Via della Rocca numero quattro—the child said, dropping into fluent Italian with barely a trace of American.

—How long have you been in Italy then?—

—Don't know. A long time.—

—Do you go to school here?—

—Yes.—

—Dalle suore, nevvero?—put in the man, smiling and nodding, proud of the child, pinching her cheek.

—Do you like it at school?—

—It's okay. But it's vacation now. Andiamo?—

—Si, meglio di si, sennò la mamma si preoccupa. Mother weill be vorriedd, eh?—

—Very good.—

Barbara smiled at him and the man laughed.

—No, not good.—

—You will have a meal with me tomorrow? Man-jare c-un me douma-ni, si?—

—Si, si, grazie signora, molto gentile. Tenk you, tenk you.—

When they had gone Barbara walked across the piazza and picked up the evening's torch stump before returning to the hotel.

On the next three evenings Barbara, the fire-eater and the child ate together after his performance. Barbara did not ask either his name or the name of the child, and they did not ask hers. She did not probe any further into their present lives, but encouraged the child's memory of America. She did not ask the fire-eater for his memories: in any case, his English and her Italian were so poor that they would not have been able to talk. The man smiled, nodded a lot, and Barbara smiled and nodded to him and talked to the child. She judged by the relish with which they fell upon the meal that they were poor. She wondered if the income of the whole group was merely the money he collected from his spectacle. She wondered what the mother of the child was like, she wondered—

All right, she wondered. But that is not the point, is it? I thought, I hoped I was alone, writing about Barbara; but as soon as you shut the book and rose from the leather armchair, you replaced him: I picture a you in my mind, a friend, a current lover, an enemy. And if there is no real you, you return suddenly, faceless, with a pale dome of thinning hair spotlighted by the standard lamp placed next to the chair, surrounded by darkness, as if on a stage. Someone has to read these pages. I thought I wielded the power because I invent the story but in fact the life of my words, the neutral of Barbara and the fire-eater are mere conductors, potential light: I need you, to turn on the switch. Words and events are not enough, however live the words might be, however carefully manipulated the events. Without you neither Barbara nor the words are more than black decorating white, and I, struggling with both, am as useless as a plug without a socket. Someone has to read: I can play with the story, twist the copper hair this way and that, but you have the final word.

The mystery lies neither in the story itself, predetermined by the labels and juxtapositions on the first page, nor in my writing of it: I can only write this, however much I toy with alternatives. I am as constrained by my self as by each word I am led to choose by what I am, and the sense of infinite possibility that was mine before I began, narrows itself down to the single story I write as much as to the single life I lead: they are identically limited. There is no other story of Barbara or of the fire-eater. It is as much a dream for me to think that tomorrow I will sit and write of a glamorous Barbara as it is for me to imagine I am other than what I am. No, the mystery lies in what you do, the mystery is reading, not writing; it is while you read that possibility is limitless and Barbara is real, though she may exist without you, like a collapsed puppet. You, not I, have the strings in your hand to bring her to life. I have only words—

Barbara guards her resources carefully not to have to stint her guests in the evening and during the next three days the day is all preparation: she forgoes all the excursions she had planned; she does her sight-seeing as if her eyes had acquired the clarity of a prescription lens: all is sharply in focus, clearly defined— she sees the details of the mosaic in San Clemente as if it were a few feet away and level with her eyes, not rising above her so that she has to crane her neck and head well back. When she returns to the hotel, she does not lie on the bed restless and weary. No, she lies on her side, not seeing the crack on the ceiling, and sleeps deeply for a couple of hours. She wakes to be refreshed by a shower and newly laundered clothes. A transformation. A pathetic transform- ation brought about by love; if you and I were not so cynical, we would weep at the sight. As it is, we laugh as she waddles in her absurd clothes to meet the man she loves: a fire-eater. As she gazes, her brown eyes small behind the thick lenses, at the absurd performance in front of her. She has almost forgotten, she has willed herself to forget, as she contemplates the man (thank God for the specs that hide the numb stare of love) that tomorrow is the last night, that all that lies ahead for her is an uncomfortable journey and Dunmow in Essex. But it can't be, I say to myself—perhaps you say to me—can't something happen to make her lastingly happy? And we toy with some drama: even the drama of death would bring relief. If the plane crashed, if a car should run her over, if the *scippatori* who are lying in wait for her should by accident knock her over, somehow kill so that she does not have to return. But we know there is no drama. In fact the fire-eater and child, though happy to have a free meal, are increasingly irritated by her presence, by the ritual meal she offers them. They wish she would go. The next evening there is to be a party in their *quartiere,* and the fire-eater is to perform at it and make that his contribution to the evening. They hope the *zitella,* the spinster, will have gone by the night they return to Piazza Navona. If she hasn't they will change their venue. So when Barbara comes eagerly to Piazza Navona on her last evening, they are not there. She waits for them, she waits for them, thrusting to the back of her mind, to the furtherest corner of her heart the fear that they will not come, the knowledge that she will not see him again. Are you tempted to make Barbara remember the address given by the child, to watch her as she goes there, compelled by her need to see him again, just once more? Are you tempted to show her, standing in the shadows, unnoticed by the noisy happy street party, looking once more on the man seated on a chair, chatting to a big blonde woman whose loud voice is carried over the noise, whose American accent reveals her as the mother of the child, the mistress of the man? But no.

Barbara sat paralysed at her table, unable to move. She sat and waited while the crowd surged and shifted, while they increased and gradually diminished, until the evening had worn itself into night, and the waiters, yawning and bad-tempered with weariness, began to assemble table and chairs to remove them indoors. She sat and waited until a waiter came up and said:
—Si chiude, signora.—Then she paid for the untouched *granita* that had melted to tepid coffee and walked back through the night

(and we think, oh please you mugger, please you killer, come out of the shadows, thrust your knife into her. But no, only carefree *scippatori,* youths for whom stealing is a game, to her hotel, to her room where the crack in the ceiling seemed to cast shadows. She undressed in the dark and lay on the bed staring at the ceiling for some time, then switched on the light and picked up her Bible.

Il Bell'Uomo

Barbara saw him first on a Wednesday evening. October being Mary's month, Barbara always made arrangements to be taken from the home for physically handicapped where she lived to the small Victorian church nearby, for Rosary and Benediction. That day she had arrived late: Ernie, who had worked for the home since he was a boy, showed his resentment at this extra October duty by invariably collecting her at the last minute on the first Wednesday of the month; once he had made his point, he would return to his grumbling kindness and allow plenty of time.

She was wheeled in and up to her place as the first decade came to an end, and as the monotone dialogue between priest and faithful continued, Barbara put the brakes on and looked up: her eyes were immediately held by a man sitting in the front pew by the west side of the altar. He was the most good-looking man she had ever seen. A head of angelic perfection, human manliness and boyish delicacy; a profile that had neither the full-lipped sensuality of Michelangelo's David, nor the hard masculine beauty of a Greek Poseidon, nor did it resemble a Raphael angel, and yet gave the same impression of something superhumanly beautiful. Barbara could not take her eyes away from his face, as his lips moved in response to the first part of the Ave, and his hands lay still and quiet in his lap, probably holding a Rosary. The whole congregation must be looking at him, she thought; yet when she looked around, everyone was pensively answering with the Santa Maria. She tried to turn her attention to the prayer but could not avoid resting her eyes on him from the position at the very front of the main aisle.

On the next three Wednesdays, though not on Sundays, the man was there kneeling and sitting in the same pew: He seemed to have a place tacitly reserved for him, as Barbara had. By the end of the month the perfection of his features had imprinted itself on her mind. Every detail of posture and manner, though full of devotion, left traces of ambiguity as if such perfection had no need, almost no right to the balm and tranquillity of worship. Barbara looked forward to the end of the devotions and the end of the disturbing presence, but when she arrived at the ten o'clock Mass on the first Sunday in November, he was there.

As the weeks went by, and Christmas rolled into the New Year and the New Year slowly moved towards Ash Wednesday and Lent, Barbara's discomfort increased; she became sure the man was watching her. She reasoned with herself that it was impossible, that her imagination was suddenly playing tricks on her, there was nothing, nothing at all except a feeling: the man never seemed to look in her direction when she looked at him, and her impression that his eyes dwelt on her while she was trying to concentrate on the rite that was taking place at the altar must surely be wrong: unlike her, he had to turn his head to see her.

The Sunday before Ash Wednesday Barbara succeeded in changing the time when she would be taken to Mass. It had been a slow process that had required the utmost tact and diplomacy with the Principal of the Home who was kindness itself but could not, obviously, give in to every whim of those of whom she took such good care. As she so rightly said: 'What would happen if everyone suddenly decided that they did not want to follow the time-table so carefully worked out for them, especially when it catered for a special need that was not the general policy of the Home?' She reached the church in time for the nine o'clock service: the place the man always occupied was filled by a child, and Barbara prayed with a fervour she had lacked for months and returned home light-hearted. On Ash Wednesday her peace was shattered. The man was present at the service, and when Barbara was wheeled up to submit to the cross of ash on her forehead she saw him just in front of her. He turned down the aisle after the cross had been marked and brushed past her. She received the ashes as the thought penetrated her mind like a falling meteor: 'He's the devil.' It took her some time to laugh and dismiss the notion. She hoped, oh how she hoped that he would not be there at Mass on Sunday. But when she arrived in time for the nine o'clock she saw him, his beautiful head bowed in prayer, the face hidden behind his long hands, the beauty in some absurd way a contradiction of the attitude of devotion. Barbara was frightened: she could not dismiss it as her imagination. He was there because she was there. He wanted something from her.

The man knelt and sat opposite her, silent and demanding, and during the next few weeks Barbara's conviction grew that she must somehow escape from him, and her need to avoid him demonstrated to her how imprisoned she was. Barbara had decided to go into a Home when her parents had grown old and had begun to find it difficult to look after her needs: with the same stubbornness that had helped her make the most of her twisted body, she had concluded that she did not want her disability to be a burden on anyone, and had been immensely happy in the Home, where she did not have to make any effort she did not feel was well within her scope to make. Gradually, as the wheelchair was there, an attendant was always at hand, and the crutches had been an effort however strong her arms had become, though she had not been a wheelchair case when admitted, Barbara used it more and the crutches less.

And now: she simply could not go to the Principal yet again and say that she wanted to change church, that she wanted to change the time, or that she no longer wanted to go to church . . . and yet not to go seemed the only solution; she had to stop going, she had to stop seeing him week after week. Then all her problems would be resolved. If he did not want anything, if it was all fruit of her imagination, he would simply disappear from her life. If he did want something, the Home was fortress against all kinds of invasions, and he would not be able to reach her.

Easter had already sung its song of praise when Barbara braced herself to face the Principal and make her request. The man had been present at that Maundy Thursday rite of the washing of the feet, and the Friday ceremonies of the Cross, at the late night celebrations of the Vigil on Holy Saturday. He had been there, and had brushed past her as she was wheeled to the altar to receive the host, to kiss the cross, to receive the host. It could not go on: Barbara felt, and tried to laugh it off, that she would go mad; yet he was there, and the only escape from him was not to return to the church. She could anticipate the Principal's disapproval and her probing questioning, just as she knew that she would neither understand nor dismiss her explanation if she were to give the real one (and how could she?), a psychiatrist would be brought in to discuss the matter with her. What was she to say? What lie would satisfy the Principal and permit her to regain peace? Her mind was so full of the absurdity of the truth—perhaps she should see a psychiatrist?—that it remained blank when she tried to think of some reasonable excuse why she should no longer want to go to church when all her adult life it had been the central point of each passing week. She smiled drily at herself at the thought of the Principal assuming it was a crisis of faith and insinuating that it really was about time she grew up as regards her religion.

Her mind was a blank wall when she knocked on the door, sat down awkwardly in the chair made to receive bodies afflicted with her disabilities, and it remained blank as the Principal's voice began to question her, until the wall was abruptly pulled away and Barbara felt as if windows had been flung open and cold clean air allowed to enter the unbearably stuffy room of her mind: she would escape from her. Barbara forgot truth and lie and the reason why she had come to speak to the Principal, and let the strange elation possess her: she would escape from her. Not only from the routine Sundays. She would escape from the Home. As she spoke the words 'I am going to leave the Home' everything seemed to fall into place, and to become luminously clear.

The Principal laughed gently, unmockingly and unmistakably full of pity: 'I understand you, I understand your need to leave. I was expecting this for some time now. Don't think I haven't noticed your unhappiness and restlessness. But my dear girl, what will you do? Where will you go? Do you realize that here you have all the help your body needs? And you know how many of your mental needs we have striven to cater for. I am sure you would not have come to see me if you did not have a plan of action, so to speak. Would you like to tell me about it?' Barbara did not know where it came from: it was as if she had been thinking about leaving for months. Without hesitation she outlined plans she had no idea she had in mind. She realized, she told the Principal, that she could not leave immediately; she would first of all intensify the physiotherapy she had grown so lazy about, to see whether her body could not re-learn to cope with more of her needs; at the same time she would take courses, typing and shorthand, whatever would permit her to earn a living. She knew she could do it. She knew she would do it, because she had to escape from the man, from the Home, from the Principal. She also knew the Principal would indulge her, not because she felt Barbara had any chance of success, but simply because it would relieve her tension. With a guile she did not know she possessed she used this knowledge. Her sister lived far, her parents were long dead, Barbara had very little private means, but she knew now that she would not employ them as she had planned, to give her sister's children a 'start in life'. No, they would be used for her own start in life. As she walked out of the Principal's room dragging her twisted body on its crutches, the limpidity of her vision persisted. She walked down the long passage, out into the beautiful grounds and let herself fall on the damp grass, and smiled into the pale blue sky and the transparent clouds. Then she began to cry.

Barbara renounced any idea of changing her Sunday routine: it would give the Principal too much food for thought and she would be bound to reach the wrong conclusion if, after announcing a plan to leave, Barbara also asked not to be taken to Mass. Instead she worked out that it would be possible for her to ask quite naturally in a few months' time, perhaps after her yearly September holiday with her sister Bridget, that she should make her own way to church on crutches, as a good form of exercise to cement her efforts to increase her mobility. Nobody would know whether she did in fact go. Barbara felt the childishness of her proposed deception and resented the mesh of care woven around her that made it necessary.

The summer was stifling: heat hung over the home like a gas, open doors and windows did not awaken the whisper of a draught to move the air. Barbara withdrew from her Home mates into her small room, where she would lie on the hard bed for hours, repeating exercises the physiotherapist had taught her until, sweat and tears mingling down her face, she would fall into an exhausted sleep. For the first time in her life she lost the heaviness that seems the inevitable accompaniment of a body forced to limit its activity. The Principal watched, but could do nothing: all her efforts were met with sweet-tempered iciness by Barbara. When she was not on her bed, Barbara sat at the desk forcing her fingers to the keyboard of a typewriter, forcing her mind to concentrate on the text books of subjects she had chosen for exams in the late autumn.

Barbara's sister Bridget had married two years after Barbara had begun living in the Home, and her first child, Barbara's namesake, was born shortly after. Ever since then, except for the autumn six years later when Bridget's second child was born, she had spent a week to ten days with them. There had been times when Barbara had felt this tradition to be a bind: her life had run on such smooth rails that she had started to look upon any change as an intrusion. This year Barbara confronted within herself a painful desire to see her sister, her husband and the two children. She sat at her desk in the strangely implacable heat of that summer and her eyes slipped over the words of the text book in front of her as memories of forgotten past holidays spent first in the small flat and then in the light suburban home replaced memories of her own childhood, and these in turn made room for strikingly clear pictures of her sister's children, until she yielded to sleep in the still air and the silence, with a strange melancholy as if by this sleep she were missing an opportunity, and yet unable to resist the drug. She invariably woke up with the clear perception of the man's face bent over her, as though he had come to wake her.

She became aware that her determination to leave, which wavered at times when her crippled body remained stubbornly unresponsive to the exercises, and the concentration on the text books resembled that of a small fly endlessly hitting its small head against the hard transparency of glass, endlessly climbing up a window, seeking an outlet into the air, and always slipping down again, that determination would be revived and strengthened by the presence of the man on Sundays. He never looked at her, and no longer even brushed past her on his way up or back from the altar rails, but once Barbara had yielded to the weekly contemplation of the perfection of his head and profile, the beauty of those hands into which the face would be buried in times of silent prayer, her fear and terror were replaced by an equally irrational perception of him not as demonic but as angelic. By the time her sister was due to come to take her away, the man had become the mainspring behind her efforts, as if by leaving she would not lose him. She did not acknowledge it to her rational mind, but she was now convinced that in some way he was making the fantastic demand that she should leave the Home.

Bridget brought her young son when she came to collect her in the second week of September. Although Barbara had been fond of the children, she had never allowed her feelings to go below the surface, and was disturbed to feel as though a stone had hit her ribcage and stopped her from breathing for a second or two when she caught sight of Bridget walking into the common room where she was waiting for them, holding Harry's hand—and the child on his best behaviour looked curiously around at the more or less crippled bodies arranged around the room performing different tasks. Bridget greeted her with the usual gentle briskness, pushed the child forward to kiss his aunt, picked up the case as Barbara heaved herself up on to her crutches and began the slow progress down the corridor to the entrance, to the car. During the long drive, as the child gazed out of the window at the moving countryside, then stretched himself on the seat and fell into a deep sleep, the two sisters discussed how and when Barbara could carry out her plans. Barbara wondered why she had been so hesitant about writing, Bridget seemed to accept her decision without question. She was immediately full of schemes for finding her work, for finding somewhere to live—she could of course live with them, but Bridget felt sure that Barbara would prefer to live on her own. The two sisters talked and laughed, moved from other topics back to her question, sat in comfortable silence for stretches and Barbara, puzzled again by the ease with which she seemed to cry now, had to fight to keep her tears back. Only when they had arrived, exhausted by the long drive, had eaten a welcoming meal, and sat talking for a while and then had gone to bed, did she allow herself to cry.

After the first week, when she lived in limbo, taken over by the energy and enthusiasm of her sister's household, Barbara began to miss the Home and question her decision. Now that she was not there, her determination wavered again and again. She could not understand the impulse that had driven her to decide, and the idea that it should be the man presented itself to her mind in its complete absurdity. She watched her sister and toyed with the idea of telling her about him—then shrank from the thought, not so much for any incredulity she might arouse, but in fear, as if she would lose him by speaking, as if any articulation, even just a physical description, would make him vanish—but she wondered at herself: perhaps the man did not exist? Perhaps she suffered from hallucinations? At moments he seemed to recede from her mind, and she was glad: in the absence of a tangible sight of him the original ambiguity was beginning to make her feel uncomfortable again.

During the week after her return to the Home with definite plans—she would leave at Christmas and stay with her sister while they looked for somewhere for her to live close by so that Bridget would be at hand to help; Ian had already started to make tentative inquiries for suitable secretarial positions, and a school had said they would bear her in mind should a vacancy arise for a switch-board operator—Barbara's mind seemed to her a smooth, gloss-painted hollow of precarious serenity: the ambiguity that the memory of the man's presence left in her had grown, and she had swayed between feeling that her original interpretation was correct and accusing herself of morbidity, hallucinations, psychological instability. At the very back of her mind, behind all thought, interpretation and rationalization, she longed to look upon the perfect features once more, but this was coupled with a fear even greater than the longing, and she remained so determined to bypass the church that she had discontinued the arrangements to be taken to church on Sundays. She had explained that she now felt strong enough to walk the short distance, and the Principal had agreed to the change. Ernie had pretended delight, and shown his concern by offering to pick her up after the service, for the first weeks at least. Barbara was touched and wondered whether the concern had always been there and she had remained blind to it all these years.

She embarked on her first walk on the first Sunday in October, so tense with determination that the crutches were stiffer and more unwieldy and her body heavier than they had ever been. She swung slowly past the church, not looking at the groups of people that were entering it, at the children running around postponing the moment when they would have to leave the sunshine, and moved to the common nearby where she sat on a bench, trembling from exhaustion. She watched people intently, forcing herself to think of their possible lives in order not to think of her own, concentrating on faces and movements and activities to stop the sobs rising in her chest in waves. The face of the man was a nightmare of demands and contradictions. It rose in front of her, obliterating the Sunday life of the common, dulling the sound of games and footsteps through leaves. She could not not see him. She rose in fear from her seat and retraced her steps in fear, trembling and unaware of her body swinging along carried by the crutches and the strength of her arms. She reached the church as the priest received the offerings from the people, but the man was not there. Barbara looked at the vacant seat filled by a fat elderly lady wearing a precariously perched fur hat, and her vision played strange tricks: the habit of turning her eyes slightly from the altar and looking upon the long fingers, the bowed head, the reverent posture, the profile lips as they moved in response to the priest, made his image flicker in front of her like that of a cinematic ghost. She knew she would not see him again, but refused to believe it: she returned to the church on Wednesday for the Rosary and Benediction, then on Sunday, again on the following Wednesday, and each time the hope that he would be there would carry her as she struggled, in the persistent warmth of that autumn, to reach the church. A variety of people seemed to have taken over the seat, a child, a fat lady, a plump and plain teenager, a tall imposing woman. He had gone. He had gone. He had gone.

At the end of October the weather broke and Barbara stopped going to church. Her body still did the daily round of daily exercises, her fingers acquired a surprising skill on the typewriter, the forefront of her mind applied itself to the text books—though she knew she would fail in the exams—but the reason why she was doing all this had slipped away from her: she was a stone or a shell existing in a dark room, and in the darkness there were no days or weeks. Occasionally she wondered that the absence of what had been such a faint and ambiguous presence should have shut her in a room so dark. But she could no longer reach out and open the door, and did not really believe that beyond that dark room there was any light.

She was faintly surprised when her sister came to collect her and she saw that all the arrangements for leaving had been made, that all her accumulated belongings had been packed, that she was about to say goodbye to the Principal and her crippled companions; that she had said goodbye and was sitting in the car being driven away in the grey light of a winter's day.

Objects

There was the watch given to her by her parents when she was twelve—'very old make'—she had been shocked to hear when she had taken it to be repaired. As she walked home that time after entrusting the watch to the shop, she was suddenly panic-stricken. What if instead of mending it they looked at it and told her that it was beyond repair? What if they said they had mended it, but it should keep breaking again and again? The fear and anger at the thought were totally disproportionate to the object. She could easily get another. She did not even have the problem of money, she had accumulated so much in the past few years. In fact she knew she looked a little strange with a plain, child's watch on her wrist, when her life nowadays required her to be always at her most elegant and well-dressed. She wore it all the time. Every night, when her work required her to take it off, the fear would begin as she removed it. It was the only time she thought her work less than satisfactory.

Then there was the pen. It was a fountain pen, again it had been given to her, this time by her mother just before she had married. It had been the only object she had called her own throughout the long time she had stayed with her husband: she had sellotaped on it a piece of paper with her name. After the birth of her child she had not been able to afford to buy ink for it. When her brother had come to see her, she had not begged him to help her by giving her money, but she had been compelled to ask for a bottle of ink, and after that her brother would send her one periodically, though he himself never came to see her again. They only kept in touch through this bottle of ink every six months or so. Although she had not communicated with him when she had left her husband and embarked on her work, he had somehow found out where she was and the bottle of ink still arrived.

There was the missal. She had found it in a church in a small

town where she had gone to meet someone who did not want to
see her in London. She thought that was strange at the time—it is
so much easier to hide in London. When she had met him she had
understood—it is also much easier to escape in a big city—and had
been frightened. When she had finally managed to get away from
him—she suspected that he had actually relaxed his vigilance
because he was bored with her, and was surprised at her annoyance
at this thought—she had returned to the church and collected the
missal. It was an old book, published in 1845 (approval for publi-
cation given on the 25th of September 1845 by Thomas, Bishop of
Cambysopolis and Nicholas, Bishop of Melipotamus, coadjutor),
that had belonged to someone called Thomas Lowler in 1890, who
had bought it, or at least signed it, on the 19th February of that
year. At the back, inside the cover, it said:

Should this book
be by accident left
in the church the
owner would be obliged
if other people
would let it remain
there!!!

The writing was old-fashioned, obviously the same person's who
had put the signature and date inside the front cover. It was a tiny
book, with etchings of the Good Shepherd, the Lamb of God and
of a priest raising the host at the consecration. She had put a rubber
band around it, and had placed it in the inside compartment of her
bag. She had only taken it out to transfer it from bag to bag, and
had never gone further than look at the pictures. She planned to
return to the church one day and replace it where she had found
it.

There was also a pair of glasses. She had met the person who
had finally made her leave her husband when he had sat on her
glasses one day, and had offered to pay for them to be repaired.
She had celebrated leaving her husband and the life they had shared
by pretending, with the other, that she had lost her glasses. He told
her she should have contact lenses and had given her a pair as a
present. The lenses changed her life completely, and though she

had soon left the giver of the gift, who wanted her to divorce and marry him, the lenses helped her in establishing herself in her career, where looks and class were so important. She kept her glasses in the same compartment of her bag where the missal was, and she went through the same routine of transferring them to whatever bag she was carrying around at whatever point of her day and night. But she had not put them on since the day she had claimed to have lost them.

In her fortieth year she had her bag snatched from her in the street, in broad daylight, by a couple of youths on a motor-bike, who thundered past her and knocked her down. They must have been the same age as her own child, fourteen or fifteen. She knew the police would not be able to find it, so she put an advertisement in the paper for a high reward on the return of her bag with the contents, and remained dazed and bewildered with anguish until it was returned to her. The glasses were lost, but by some miracle the missal was there. The rubber band had been removed, and the picture of the Good Shepherd had been torn, but it was all there. She decided to put it in a safe in the bank. When later that year the optician advised her that she should no longer wear contact lenses—her eyesight was deteriorating rapidly and she was now in need of reading glasses—she set out to find someone to marry.

On the day of her second wedding she received a telegram telling her that her brother had died. A few days later the last bottle of ink she was to receive from him arrived. She buried it, unused, side by side with the fountain pen, at the bottom of the large garden.

It took her husband some years to discover that the watch his wife wore did not work. He realized that she always asked him the time, never looked at the watch although she never took it off; then noticed that she wore it even in the bath, careful not to put her left arm in the water. Yet she changed the strap as soon as it began to be worn. He decided to give her a new watch on their wedding anniversary. Her silence and occasional oddities had strangely endeared her to him after he had overcome the dislike he had felt when he discovered that she had seduced him and lured him into believing she was someone who could satisfy all his desires.

*

She seemed grateful for the new watch. Smiling she took off her old one and replaced it on her wrist by the new one (there was a faint grey mark where the old watch had been. She had not taken it off for years). Then she took her child's watch and buried it in the garden, next to the bottle of ink and the pen.

A few weeks later her husband was surprised to hear her talking on the phone: he had not heard it ring, and she never phoned herself. She agreed to meet one day on the following week, promised to bring the book with her and apologized for a torn picture. The day before the arranged meeting, she went to the bank and withdrew the missal from the safe. It was in a brown, anonymous envelope, and she did not bother to remove it. Her husband, puzzled but not daring to question her, drove her to the station in time to catch the early train, collected her late that evening; the next morning woke, chilled, to find her curled up with her back to him, her joined hands between her thighs, her limbs cold and already beginning to stiffen.

Experiment with Time

1

Time ran out: I snatched the trilby and the long red woollen scarf from the entrance table and followed him into a blustery autumn air, shutting the door behind me and slipping the key into the pocket of the knickerbockers. He was running down the tree-lined avenue, kicking up a dust of brittle brown and yellow leaves. I could see the sole of his sandals; he jogged with his whole body bent forward at an almost dangerous angle: to keep his balance, he held his knees close together and threw his shins and feet sideways. I would have no trouble catching up with him to demand an explanation, he obviously couldn't run much faster, impeded further by the black soutane which he held high with both hands; and I was in tip-top condition, barely using one-third of my energy as I trotted in comfortable running shoes.

The wide avenue was asphalted, and the occasional Rolls, Bentley or Daimler came towards us, slowed down as Time passed them and gathered speed to pass me. I caught glimpses of dark-haired men and blonde women, and thought how glad I was not be cooped up but running behind Time in the autumn air: a strong wind whipped the trees, the branches cringed and cried multicoloured leaves; the sky hid behind large comfortable clouds and the sun teased the earth and the tall white-washed houses on either side with its game of peek-a-boo. My lungs expanded, my pulse was steady; my heart beat regularly, if a fraction fast. My feet beat the pavement and crushed leaves with determination: for a minute I was even grateful to Time for dragging me out in pursuit of him.

A car appeared where the avenue narrowed on the horizon. It was quite small, a popular rather than an exclusive make. There was a trailer attached. When it was level it swerved on the road, and turned, drew up alongside me and parked a little ahead. I reached it as the door of the caravan opened and an exquisitely dressed woman stepped on to the pavement. She smiled at me, removed a pin from her hair and let it tumble on her shoulders, danced as she slipped out of her red and gold dress and stood in front of me in a fur jacket, black stockings and high-heeled ankle boots, stretching out her hand to take mine and draw me in. I looked ahead. Time stood still, staring at me, a grin of mockery on his pink-cheeked, pudgy face. As I stepped in I saw him settle with his back against one of the trees and take out a book. He was odious.

The woman was beautiful and desirable and for a while I forgot Time waiting for me with his book. The trailer shook with our energetic games: we were very close. So close I decided to tell her.

'I want to kill Time,' I murmured into her soft hair as we lay in wonderful exhaustion.

'I know what you mean,' she replied, and we began another more gentle game.

'He owes me an explanation,' I explained to her afterwards.

'I know. He never explains to anyone,' she said. She was so understanding and beautiful I wanted to play again. But I pulled myself up short.

'Time is now ripe. With your help I can beat him, I can kill him. We must draw up a plan of attack. Is he still there?'

She looked through the pale venetian blinds and leapt to her feet: 'No, no, shit fuck, he's gone!'

'Now we've lost him. What are we to do?'

It was childish, but I felt near to tears. To lose him, when I almost had him in my grasp. I couldn't help blaming her, and we quarrelled violently; the caravan shook as we threw plates and glasses at each other, then chairs and finally fought over the table. We were having a real tug of war when she suddenly slackened her hold on two of the legs. It hurled me backwards against the back-end of the trailer.

'Look,' she shouted, pointing at the window just above me. There was Time flying past.

'Quick, we mustn't lose him again.'

I jammed the trilby on my head and wrapped the scarf around my neck, and she slipped on her fur and boots.

'You're naked,' she said as we stumbled out.

'Never mind that,' I said looking around, 'this is war, a war against Time,' I shouted and took her hand as we caught a glimpse of him flying above the bare trees.

'He's not going to escape us. We'll catch him, we'll beat him, we'll kill him. We'll mark him, we'll have him at our disposal, he'll be at out beck and call.'

'We'll waste him,' she screamed.

We ran down the narrowing avenue, looking up at him. He dipped and cavorted maliciously ahead of us; he dived and came close to landing and then took off like a kite caught in a gust of wind; the black soutane that had so impeded his movement spread out, filled like a sail and lifted him high. I saw his laughing face, both innocent like a child being thrown in the air, and an old man leering, knowing. She stuck her tongue at him and hurled abuse as we ran. I was glad of her coarse yelling, though I could never have used such language. I saw again how beautiful and desirable she was and almost stopped. But I was chasing Time. I let go of her hand and heard her shouting still as I ran faster than I'd ever run in my life, to keep him in sight through the thinning branches. Until he gave one last mocking dip, like a bow, and disappeared into the thick carpet of winter clouds. I stood panting, cursing myself: I should have got him when he was running like a knock-kneed girl.

2

I must have run very fast and very far because when I looked around I was in a vast plain and the woman was nowhere to be seen. In the distance I could just distinguish the outline of stark trees of what might have been the avenue or might have been a wood. The snow was knee-deep and swirled against my legs in an icy breeze. It was cold; and I was naked save for the trilby and the red scarf. Time had exposed me to this: I'd find him, he'd regret everything he'd done to me ... Remembering that the way to survive the cold is to keep moving, I started to walk towards the only visible alteration in the landscape, and stopped when the cold had reduced me to a state beyond numbness, a state of complete indifference. If I couldn't somehow cover at least the most delicate member, I'd no longer care whether I did catch up with Time . . . Perhaps I could make a pair of trunks with the red scarf I had been fingering, uselessly wrapped around my neck? I passed it between my legs, holding one end in front, wound the rest once around my waist, tucked what I was holding inside the belt, and I had a breech-cloth. The scarf was so long that I could even wear the other end over the left shoulder, to afford it a measure of protection from the icy wind blowing from that direction. It was as well there was no longer any feeling in my feet: all I had to do was to force my legs to keep them moving.

Warmed a little by the clothing of my nakedness I walked on defiantly, thinking I'll catch up with Time if it kills me, and kill him. I'll kill the bastard, I'll beat him senseless. This refrain, repeated rhythmically in my brain, kept me going until I reached the edge of the wood. But it was hopeless: the wood was an extension of the desolation behind me, the trees dressed in icicles, the shrubs buried in snow, and no sign of life.

The falling of night began to be accompanied by the silent fall of large flakes, which made the air a touch warmer, and my problem greater. Where could I shelter? Didn't mountain-climbers make hide-outs from packed snow? But my frozen fingers refused to obey me.

I leant against the side of a tree that was not covered in snow, and wept. I had let Time slip by, when I could have caught up with him. And Time was no more. Nor would I have another chance to seek him, bound to death by my foolish pursuit of him. If only I had been wearing the thick jumper and woollen knicker-bockers. If only she was with me, with her warm fur and hot body . . . the running shoes . . . the soft thickness of the fur, so carelessly cast aside in our game . . . the sheltering caravan . . . the bed: it had blankets, though we had not needed them . . . never to play games again. To die in an ice-cold wood and all because of Time. The bastard, the bastard—I shook myself and opened my eyes. Just a little distance away, Time marched on, looking ridiculous with his black soutane trailing in the snow; but I couldn't laugh. He seemed unaware of me, absorbed like a child in a game. He goose-stepped steadily past me, deep into the wood, and I shut my eyes.

3

I woke as if the thought, must find Time, had been an electric shock, and sat up: I was in a low bed, in a low-roofed room that smelt of baking bread. I could hear rain crashing on the roof and gurgling in the gutter, and a more distant roar, as if there was a river near by. The darkness was lit by the fire of a large oven. A shadow moved back and forth in front of it.

'I must find Time,' I said. My voice had gone, what came out was a croak.

'No,' the shadow said as she came near me.

'Eat,' she said, handing me a loaf.

'But my fingers could not grasp the bread.

'Frostbite,' she said and sat on the bed. She was an old woman, wrapped in shawls, her face inscribed with lines. When she smiled I saw she was toothless, but her eyes were bright. She broke the bread and fed me as long as my stiff jaws allowed me to chew. I lay back exhausted as she stepped back to the oven, returned with a cup of hot water: gently she held my head in her gnarled hand and the cup close to my lips. I sipped, drank thirstily, ate a little more bread.

'Thank you,' I croaked.

'Sleep,' she said. And I slept.

The chatter of birds woke me. Sunlight poured in from the one window and danced on the floor from the wide open door next to the oven. I looked around but I was alone. I tried to get up: it was as if parts of my body were no longer there. All feeling had gone from the fingers except the thumb and forefinger of the left hand; the feet were senseless stumps. This damage Time had done to me. How I hated him. Yet even as I thought I found I had no strength to hate. I had no strength at all, and could only lie feebly waiting for her return.

'My scarf,' I said when her shadow darkened the doorway.

'Yes. And your hat.' She beamed her toothless smile and I was stirred by its tenderness. She rummaged under the bed and took

out my dusty possessions, fed me bread; weak tears streamed down
my face, and she wiped them away with her rough fingers, in
silence. She was extraordinarily comforting.

'Don't fight against Time,' she chanted as I was falling asleep
once more.

'No,' I mumbled.

'But play for him.'

'Yes,' I said.

'Spare Time,' she rocked me in my sleep.

'And you will find him and keep him.'

'Serve Time,' she sang as she fed me bread while I learnt to use
the two fingers that had not died.

'And you will have the fullness of him.'

Take Time,' was her lay as she led me to the river. Cuckoos
called in the wood, and I followed her on my knees, wearing the
trilby, with the long red scarf around my neck, dragging the stumps
that had once been feet and shins.

'And he'll be your very own sweet Time, without end,' she
murmured as we sat by the bank and looked on the water: Time
flowed by on his back, weighed down by the saturated black
soutane, and on his face the mischievous smile of a child.

Eurydice

Eurydice smiled faintly:

—Of course, this is the place. I recognize it, I have always
known it, it has always been there, the backdrop to all my living.
Everything I've done, been or said has been an attempt to avoid
it.—

—I wonder why I was so frightened of it.—She tried to speak,
but no sound came: silence filled every nook and cranny like a
steady fall of snow, the stillness momentarily lifted by draughts on
her face, her hands and her legs extended in front of her. Rocks
punctuated the expanse, lit by the late twilight of a winter's afternoon that cast no shadows, reducing the landscape to a two-dimen-
sional set through which she rose to walk slowly.

—I have been like a man who panics at the sight of a white-
washed wall, fills it with figures, invents a scene, a story, adds
colours, crowds every inch with decorative motifs, doodles, anything
to hide the whiteness; that neither he, nor the master of the house,
nor the meanest slave may have to walk into the room and see a
bare wall.—

—I have rushed around filling my life with people, things, stories,
incidents, events, colours, light, sound, in an effort to paint over
the landscape. Even Orpheus . . .

—Especially Orpheus. His song, his voice, that sound from the
lyre. All seemed to say, there is no Hades. His love said, there is
no Hades.—

—But there is,—she thought with satisfaction.

She sat down, tired from the brief walk, closed her eyes and
drifted into a half-dream full of shadows: some stretched out grey
hands in greeting, some turned to her with slow smiles, others
moved past without seeing her, staring through her to a nothing

beyond. Some she recognized, though she could not put names to them, nor call out: all shared her languid peace.

—I am one of them. Thank God.—

She opened her eyes and was alone in the cool desert of grey sand and iron-stone: the shades would not intrude, they were there but need not be seen. She was alone and at peace. The only thing remaining from the world was the ache of the snake bite that made her limp as she walked in the indifferent landscape.

—I wonder why I've been so frightened of it? I wonder why I could not bear the thought of a white-washed wall? It's so peaceful, no intrusive sound, not even my own voice echoing in my ears. No song of bird or man—didn't Orpheus' song hurt? Nothing hurts here. No intrusive movement, the dancing, the never being still of slaves and gods, always doing things, making chaos, then setting it right, only to shatter it once more.—

She had little energy, and it satisfied her: no effort was required of her, she could enjoy the peace of sitting, of being in the black and grey set. If she walked, her movement disrupted nothing, not even the sand on which she stepped. She had nowhere to go, and she could be everywhere, even, she saw when she closed her eyes, in the world: she thought of Orpheus and saw him, small, far away and extremely clear, crying like a child beside the body of a woman she did not recognize as herself. She did not look for long because the brightness of the light hurt her eyes, and her lover's suffering seemed to penetrate and alter the cool underworld. But she liked to think she could, with the blink of an eyelid, summon the earth she had left, though it could not reach her.

But the grief of Orpheus filled the sky:

—What shall I do without Eurydice—he cried.

—Che farò senz' Euredice, che farò, che farò—he sang, and the lyre accompanied him in sympathy without the pluck of fingers now raised to the heavens in supplication, now violently tearing at his clothes, now joined in prayer, now childishly trying to wipe tears from his face.

—Che farò senza 'l mio amore, che farò—he sang, and the song overflowed the sky, penetrated a crack and trickled like water through the permeable earth, over impermeable rock; and soon it was made into a rivulet of sounds that fell through layers of earth and rock, down to where the shades made their sluggish way along the gravel paths of the shadowless world.

And the song in its journey lost its harmony and the tune that filled the skies and silenced the wind, halted the clouds in their course, and stilled the flights of birds as they listened in awe and tears. The tune did not find the small crack, the harmony was unable to trickle past the compact earth: only the high thin notes reached the underworld, pain distilled, and as they wailed in the cool they echoed from boulder to boulder and became a cater-wauling of sound. And the shades reeled and bowed like reeds in a strong wind at the whine; and they prostrated themselves to the ground with pale hands over ghostly ears, but were unprotected.

And Persephone too cowered under the sound, then asked Hermes to order the singer to cease the song: Orpheus could speak to Eurydice in Hades; and if she so chose, she would return with him to the blue and green world.

Immediately silence covered the underworld like a blanket and the shades raised themselves from the ground, forgetful already of the sound of pain, as Orpheus leapt from hill to hill, ran through valleys and plains, waded rivers and swam lakes to reach the gates of Hades. And the lyre on his back was light as a feather, fingers of breeze accompanied his song as he journeyed, a sweet music that quickened the heart of the earth and brought a blush to the skies, but could not reach the underworld: Pluto had moved swiftly, sending earth-spirits to close the dangerous crack.

And when Orpheus reached the gates, Pluto's servants stood waiting, bearing a hooded cloak for him: the green of his tunic, the blue of his eyes, the black of his hair, the very colour of his skin would make Hades squint as at a strong light. So muffled he slithered down the rocky slopes, raising a dust that had never been disturbed, leaving footprints on the sand that aeons would not remove.

Now without thought, Eurydice sat on a rock gazing into the indistinct light when the cowled figure came upon her. She looked at it with indifference: shades had been moving in front of her and vanished, though she had seen them with her eyes closed, in a dream.

—The head is covered—she mused. All the shades she had seen wore trailing tunics and had been bareheaded, like herself. Their hair, like hers, colourless.

—Oh, she is cold—Orpheus murmured as he knelt at her feet and took the hand lying still in the lap. And the underworld trembled as at an earthquake at the sound of a voice.

—Who is this shade that makes Hades tremble and hides in a cloak?—

Eurydice looked down on him with faint fear.

—Eurydice, return with me to the world, leave cold Hades and the stillness of non-existence—he spoke in a whisper, but the words cracked the stones all around them, and Eurydice withdrew her hands from his to cover her ears against the splitting sounds.

—The hand was warm—she thought, and was afraid to think further.

—Eurydice, Eurydice—he whispered to the cold shade.

—Is that my name?—and she remembered.

—Who are you that know my name on earth and whose touch is warm?—

—He is real—she thought in terror, and recoiled, suddenly feeling the damp air penetrate through her as if she were body; crying though still without words:—Persephone, take me away back to silence.—

—Come with me, come back with me to the world, Eurydice—Orpheus spoke again; and seeing her pale and shivering, sat by her on the rock.

—No, no—she thought, powerless against the will of the gods, as he wrapped the cloak around her. And she became flesh in the warmth: her sandalled feet and pale face became tinged with the blood that began to course in the veins, her hair darkened, her eyes brightened and filled with tears when she recognized him.

—Orpheus has defied Hades, Orpheus has rescued me from death. I must return to the earth because of this love—she thought, and she wept that she would have to re-enter the world of sound and movement.

—Eurydice, Eurydice—Orpheus whispered.

—Take me with you to the earth where there is heat and warmth and beauty—she said, weeping that she was no longer dead, and yearning to leave the grey and be with Orpheus in life.

—I am cold now in this cold world—she wept, and Orpheus cast off his cloak that it should warm her new-found body; and the movement rocked Hades, and the sight of him dazzled Eurydice; and she ceased weeping in awe.

And Orpheus played his lyre to bring life to Hades; and as he sang, the ground, wet with Eurydice's tears, sprouted tiny green grass, the light became the light of a summer's dawn, the shades paused in their meaningless wanderings. And all were made present, so that Orpheus and Eurydice saw Hades thronging with men, women and children; and the grey of their ghostly being was coloured with the light conjured up by the sweetness of Orpheus' song. And for a time, while the song lasted, all wept, remembering what could no longer be theirs; and as soon as their tears reached the ground, it sprouted a thick green down of grass.

When the song was finished, the shades smiled at Orpheus and Eurydice.

—Go—they chanted in a murmur like the memory of an echo.

—Go—they chanted, and waved at them.

—But—thundered Pluto—Orpheus, do not turn back to look at her until you've passed the gates; let her wear your cloak for warmth, but let her not feel the warmth of your body, not even a helping hand, until you are beyond our world.—

—Go—murmured the shades. And already before they had turned to leave, the rosy light of dawn faded, the grass withered, the shades vanished, and Orpheus and Eurydice were alone in the underworld.

For a while, as they trudged through the unfriendly sand and gravel, the memory of his song and his warm embrace drew Eurydice as if pulled by a current. She saw him moving with determination and certainty ahead of her, displacing stones, changing the landscape, and loved him.

Then the tempters came: a spirit breathed past her, whispering in her ear, quickly followed by others.

—Have you forgotten the pain?—
—What about the ceaseless dance?—
—The meaningless activities?—
—Your will die again.—
—What is the point of leaving Hades only to return?—
—It's inescapable.—
—But it's peace.—
—And silence.—
—There is no silence in Orpheus' world.—
—There is no peace in Orpheus' world.—
—And love is a poor, vanishing thing.—
—Already he has ceased to care. Look how he walks ahead, striding forgetful out of Hades.—

And she thought—let him turn that I may return to the unlighted world—but then—oh, but he came to Hades to bring me back to the world. Has he not won my life with his pursuit of me in death?—

Hearing a cry that was like the whimpering of a kitten, Orpheus stopped:—Eurydice—he said—I may not turn around, stay close that I may know you are all right.—

—Yes—she said.

—Stay close enough that I may feel your sweet breath—Orpheus said.

—Yes—she said. But the tempters returned.

—There is winter and ice. The grass withers and the flower fades, only Hades remains, unchanging and still.—

—Think, Eurydice, of the peace.—

—The love will die, Always it dies.—

—Oh, but while it lives, while it lives . . .

—Eurydice, it will die, one day Orpheus will turn away and the song will be silent for you.—

—He will sing to others and you will be alone.—

—Think, Eurydice, of the pain of being alone.—

—Is it not best to return to the painless world?—

—Where being alone is peace?—

—You will see Orpheus and know all he does.—

—You will be saved the pain of loving.—

—Eurydice, Eurydice, return to Hades.—

—Let him turn that I may return to the lifeless world—she

thought. But then—no—Eurydice shouted—let me be. I will live and I will love Orpheus. If he ceases to love me I will mourn in fields, at the foot of stalwart trees, But as long as he loves me I will be with him.—

Orpheus, not hearing her behind him, stopped again.

—Eurydice, Eurydice, I may not turn, if I turn I shall lose you, stay close behind me. Tell my why you cry out so and why you fall behind. Are you weary, shall we rest awhile?—

—No, no Orpheus, let's run out of Hades to the world. Let's not linger or walk, let's run. I'll keep up with you, please run, let's flee the underworld.—

Eurydice stretched out a hand, but Orpheus stepped back:—Eurydice, do not reach out to touch me, we may not until Hades is behind. But yes, let us run that I may soon hold you.—

And they ran towards the gates: the light of the world was a diamond in the semi-darkness, and they ran, scrambling up through the unyielding ground. As she ran Eurydice thought one last time:—let him turn that I may return to the unthinking world—then smiled to know she would soon be immersed in that light and Orpheus would sing to her. And Orpheus, like a child in a game, ran fast to the gate, turned to see how far she was behind him, and for a second saw her as she had been before death. But Pluto was still lord at the gates: as Orpheus opened his arms to receive her, he saw her eyes dim, the warm flesh-colour drain from her face; the cloak crumpled, empty at his feet, and Eurydice

spoke a last farewell that he could hear
but faintly now, and then turned back again
to the place where she had been.

And as the gates opened and earth spirits thrust Orpheus into the relentless light, even the lyre was silent.

While she, already cold
in death, had gone aboard the Stygian skiff.

Glass

1 Athon's Story

For some months Athon went frequently to the clearing and walked around, exploring for the first time the reflection of a whole body in movement, the gracefulness of legs raised and lowered in a canter, fascinated by the motion of arms, the smile that greeted his, trying to catch himself before turning to face himself. When his fantasy had developed into an alternative reality, the boy insisted that he enter the dome and stretched out an arm at the same time to encourage him. The door swung open into a vast round hall enclosed in glass, full of adults and children engaged in strange activities: high in the hollow of the dome men and women flew into each other's arms from trapezes; lower down women in red walked carefully across ropes stretched from end to end holding their arms out to keep their balance; below, groups of men formed themselves into human pyramids and dissolved into somersaulting figures, while near them jugglers threw green balls and plates into the air, fire-eaters exhaled flames, boys rode on single cycles, girls plied their bodies into strange neckless four-footed monsters. At the other end was a large earth-coloured mound: toddlers were scrambling all over it, squealing and laughing.

Athon stood by the door, mesmerized by the colour and movement, until a girl unfolded herself and came over.

—Can I try?—he asked after a minute, when a dark-haired boy came hurtling past on a cycle, arms extended, the tip of his tongue showing between his lips, a vertical line on his forehead from concentration.

—We must ask the giant.—Thera said, and took his hand to lead him across the hall.

—Catch—a juggler said, throwing one of the green balls.

—Pass the second ball from one hand to the other while the first is in the air—he told him throwing him a third ball.

—It's all in the timing—he added when they fell at his feet.

Athon was about to bend over to pick them up when a couple came by on a single cycle: the girl's legs were around the boy's waist, her back curved over the wheel without touching it. She skimmed the ground with her arms, gathered the two balls lying nearest to Athon, raised herself and, with one arm around the neck of the boy, handed them to Athon, then leant over and pecked his lips with hers before riding off, looking back at him over the boy's shoulder. Athon had barely time to blush before the top of the human pyramid somersaulted to the ground, ran over and dragged him to face the twelve bare-chested men, aligned in a five, four and three formation. The men smiled at Athon and the boy explained:

—Put your foot on his knee, he'll help you—and demonstrated by climbing nimbly up.

—It's all a question of balance—he told him, taking his hand when Athon had been carried to the top. He stood on one of the men's shoulders, firmly held by the calves, but still swaying dangerously.

—Give me your hands—he heard, just as he felt himself losing his balance completely; a woman hanging by her feet from a lowered trapeze took hold of him under her arms, swung him and then herself on to the platform.

—Try—she said, handing him the trapeze bar. Athon swung out.

—Let go, I'll catch you—he heard half-way across. His hands slipped and as he turned upside down he felt his ankles being taken in a firm grip and he swung high towards the platform on the other side of the dome, where two girls grabbed his outstretched arms and helped him land safely.

—You have to be supple—Thera said as they sat on the high platform, swinging their legs in rhythm and looking down on the multi-coloured activities below. The girl who had kissed him sat on the other side, occasionally brushing her foot against his.

—I'm Ramyna—she told him as Thera shinned down a rope to the ground.

—You must go now—she added, pointing to the rope.—You'll be back.—

—Don't be afraid—she laughed when he hesitated.

—I'm not—Athon said, determined not to show it.

—Can I stay?—he asked Thera when he had slid down, grazing his palms and knees on the rope.

—We must ask the giant.—Thera said, and took his hand. Ramyna came by on skates, circled once, skating backwards without looking at them, absorbed in the sway of motion.

—Let's try—Thera said, and Athon lifted her by the waist while she rested her hands on his forearms and curved her head back until it almost touched the back of her knees raised to meet it. He lowered her to the ground and she pirouetted on her toes, tilting her head to one side to pass under the arch made by their joined hands. She danced away from him on her toes, threw her body into the air holding her legs parallel to the ground, landed, pirouetted again, stretched her arms and smiling came to him, ready to be caught and held for a fraction before leaping and pirouetting again on strong legs, her arms poised at an angle that enhanced the grace of each movement, the wrists and hands relaxed, the face still, framed by a mass of dark hair, the dark eyes large, lit by a slight smile. Athon danced with her to a music of movement and joy at the power and skill of their bodies. When they stopped, Thera held his hand while he panted for breath.

—We'll build up your strength—she said as Ramyna drew near, flying on her skates, her skirt flapping, caught in the breeze of her speed. Athon's heart beat hard: he wanted to dance with her.

—Perhaps—Thera told him, knowing his wish; Ramyna skated past, fair hair swirling, and turned to look at him with eyes blue and speckled with light.

—The human form divine—Athon heard. He turned towards the voice.

—Catch—Tavis said, throwing him a foil and mask.

—Keep still and concentrate—Thera said, moving to one side to observe the fencing. The young men faced each other in a sudden deep silence: everyone had stopped and had gathered in a large circle to watch. Athon had time to notice the light brown of Tavis' eyes beneath thick brows, and the seriousness of the gaze before Tavis placed the mask over his face and got into position. Athon slipped into his mask and stood poised, unafraid. Their rapiers touched in greeting and were immediately in a game of engagements and disengagements, pointed extensions of their bodies. They darted forward on light feet, and retreated, neither managing to get past the foil of the other, gradually turning until they had changed places and Athon was looking into the hall: high in the cupola, slung along the whole diameter of the dome at right-angles to him was an intricate rope. Athon raised his eyes to strong lights directed on Ramyna, dressed in glittering red, her hair hidden by a cap, standing on a platform, about to step on to the rope.

—Touché—Tavis said, touching Athon's chest with the blunt tip of his rapier, then flicking Athon's foil from his hand.

—She is dancing—Athon said, indifferent to the defeat.

Ramyna carried nothing to help her balance, but held her arms out, her head exactly aligned with her body and her eyes looking straight ahead. She stepped from the platform, casting giant shadows on to the rounded glass roof of the dome. The rope bounced gently to complex steps and leaps as she moved across, never hesitating or trembling in momentary lack of balance. Shadows danced hugely above her, mingling and separating, changing shape and hue, accompanying her in her effortless dance of defiance to a music she only could hear in the high silence where the hum of activity below could not reach her.

Unnoticed by the spellbound crowd, Tavis clambered up the long ladder and stood on the edge of the platform, waiting to help her, and in painful slow-motion, Athon watched Ramyna stretch out a hand to reach his and immediately lose the balance that had carried her across. Petrified he saw her curl up and drop, turning like a red ball in the air charged with a scream that echoed round the hall. Athon's eyes clouded over.

—She must be alone—he heard Thera say.

—There is no touch, you see—Thera added when his eyes focused again. Athon's strength and youthful energy had gone, absorbed in the scream he had heard and the scene he had witnessed.

—You shall not see her for a while—Thera continued, taking his hand—but come, you must meet the giant.—

A child who sat on the ground, reading a book, oblivious of the multi-coloured activities that continued all around him in the hall, raised his face when Athon's and Thera's shadow darkened the page. His hair was streaked with light, his smile travelled slowly from his mouth to conquer the blue and serious eyes.

—Ramyna's child—Athon thought.

—This is Nathar—Thera said, and Athon saw that she carried a toddler on her hip, who looked at him with dark laughing eyes and wriggled impatiently in her mother's arms.

—This is Thera—the mother said, putting the child down to crawl on the floor of the dome. They walked at the pace of the baby. Athon watched Nathar put down the book, join a group of jugglers, attempt and succeed in keeping three balls in the air; but it wasn't until he was swinging high on a trapeze that Athon realized that the games Nathar played had been played by himself. And with that came the realization that though he knew himself the child who swayed on the shoulders of strong men and shinned down ropes and gloried in dance, now his body was heavy, bound by heavy bones and deprived of muscle to lift them to agile heights of movement. Bewildered he turned to Thera:

—There cannot be repetition without waste. And the pattern is repetition—Thera said smiling, watching her daughter on a single cycle, with her legs around the waist of a boy, peck Nathar's lips.

—Where is the giant?—Athon asked.

—He is here—Thera answered, pointing to the earth-coloured mound next to which they were standing. The mound moved and shook itself free of children who tumbled off laughing.

—Don't be afraid—he heard as he closed his eyes in inexplicable terror. He felt himself being lifted by some vast hand that was wind and warm air and placed on some solid surface. When his terror had subsided and he dared look, he saw he was sitting high up in the roof of the dome, on a platform that swayed in comfortable rhythm. Ramyna's foot brushed against his, and she turned to smile at him briefly.

—Look—she said, returning to gaze with total concentration at the scenes being enacted below.

2 Ramyna's Love

Ramyna had always known of the dome: Athon had returned one evening when they were very young and described the strange object in the middle of the clearing:—it must be at least eighty feet—he had said with great excitement.—It's all glass. All mirrors, I could see myself—but Ramyna already knew about it, though she had never seen it. She had been angered by Athon's discovery, and pleased that almost immediately her brother turned a handstand and invited her to a competition over who could stand on their hands longer. He didn't mention it again, and occasionally Ramyna wondered if he didn't talk about it because he had lost interest or whether it had become as much his secret as it was hers. Once, as they sat with their feet in the stream close to their home, throwing pebbles to dissemble their reflections, she began to speak of it to Thera, until she saw the look in her sister's blue eyes, and leapt to her feet to look at a flower hidden behind moss at the foot of the willow.

The dome became bigger as she grew. It was the size of a circular square the spring Athon left on his first exploration more than a few days' journey from their home in the forest, and Thera's collection of wild flowers filled every inch of wall in the room she shared with Ramyna. A little later Ramyna met Tavis, and after a summer of playful and intense love-making in hot fields and beside streams in the cool, they set up house at the other end of the forest and prepared for winter. Tavis went deep in search of dead trees to fell for logs, she gathered wood for kindling among the leaves that carpeted the ground where a few weeks before she had lain while he stroked and entered her: insects and twigs would become entangled in her black hair so that his tenderness afterwards had been to free the creatures and disentangle the debris; hers had been to wipe earth from his knees with the hem of her skirt. Together they harvested apples, pears and berries, hung tomatoes and onions, searched the soil for potatoes, sowed next year's crop; together they went to the village nearby to barter for hay to feed their few cattle through the winter, and in the evening they sat in the warmth listening to the first wind shaking last leaves from the oak trees that protected their home.

Ramyna, in a silence broken by the spluttering of the fire, wondered whether to tell her lover of the dome: as summer had progressed she had felt both a growing desire to see the dome, as if knowledge of it was no longer enough and an encounter was now important, and a wish to share her secret. She wondered if he too, who knew the forest so intimately, had seen or knew of the dome; whether it was his secret too. The thought pleased her, and she delayed speaking partly out of fear and partly from pleasure at the thought of a secret they did not know they shared.

She wondered whether the intensity of their love came of an anticipation each hoped the other had. When she sometimes caught him looking at her reflection in the dark windows with a puzzled, quizzical expression, she wondered whether he was asking himself, as she did, how and when to speak and why he should want to. She wondered whether the telling would diminish the intensity, whether closeness would be lost by such acknowledgement of closeness. This fear stopped her: but she wondered at her need to voice, her need to reveal. Sometimes she missed the sufficiency that had been hers before the summer; when Athon returned, and on a frosty evening they gathered around the fire to hear tales of his exploration of snow-covered mountain-chains far away, she envied the self-contained world of her twin. But back in the silence, walking towards their home, her hand wrapped in Tavis' and stuffed inside his pocket, she looked up at the pinched stars retreating, distant, from the cold, and knew her regret could only be momentary.

Winter had locked them in so perfectly there could be no thought of escape, and Tavis had gone to the village to buy wick for the candles they would make. Almost as soon as he disappeared into the murky morning, Ramyna found herself pulling on waterproof boots, thick coat and shawls. Icy fog hung from trees like netting, the ground was a bog of dead leaves, earth and water, the only sounds the suck slurp of mud when she lifted and lowered each foot: she knew she would reach the dome though she did not know the way.

The trees grew sparse, the path opened into a track and Ramyna was in the clearing. The top of the dome rose like a mirage above a fog which thinned into a mist and then a haze as she drew near. The temperature rose: the mirrors, reflecting weak sunlight, created an area of warmth where spring reigned. A herd of cows she could see grazing peacefully, kept the grass short, except immediately around the dome where weeds grew lush and tall. Ramyna had to part them to see her reflection. She took off coat, shawls, boots and socks and walked barefoot in the grass, circling the dome, hoping the weeds would thin out and reveal a door. She realized how inadequate her imagining had been: the dome was much larger; even the power of its reflection, which had engaged and stretched her imagination, was nothing compared to the reality. Yet in her mind it had always stood free of encumbrances, glittering constantly, surrounded by a tame lawn, in permanent summer. There had been no clouds to dull the light, no weeds to block the reflection. Now she saw that the sky played games of shadows on it; she looked from a little way and noticed that though the sides were clear, the dome top was spattered with bird droppings.

She would have to clean it, Ramyna thought, and clear it of weeds. She would have to make it correspond to her imagining. Of course, she thought as she muffled up to face the road back into winter, that was probably why she had felt such compulsion to see it. Maybe someone had tended it until recently, and she had to take over the task. The thought gave her intense pleasure.

The fog had lifted a little and the cold was hardening the ground when she entered the forest again: the crackle of wild creatures disturbed in their search for food seemed loud as her footsteps, patches of sky appeared above the trees. Ramyna strode back quickly until a sudden apprehension stopped her. Was this the moment to tell Tavis? To seek his help? In the summer and autumn even companionship and shared play had sometimes seemed too much. But the closing in of winter had made her keenly aware of distance in his evening silence; how love could be an instrument of separation, and she had contemplated the double-edged nature of it, to be close to someone in one way to be closed from each other in others. That the two words should be the same, close, closed, was a contradiction she wanted resolved. Or should she simply accept it as a necessary limitation? If she shared this, her only secret, would their closeness then exclude any closure, or would the boundaries of what they would know of each other simply change? Or would she somehow lose him in the telling? She asked herself again, why she should think to lose him, and concluded, as she had done before, that it was not so much the telling of this that made her fearful, as the voicing of anything that might alter the balance that made up their life together. How curious it was, she thought as she stepped along the now familiar path to her home, that love was the cause of so much deception, the very love that made her wish, in a way she had never before considered, for truth. Oh, there was truth between them, she thought, unwrapping shawls in the warmth, pulling off boots, unbuttoning the coat; but limited, hedged by doubts and apprehensions, by assumption, presuppositions: it could not grow unless she spoke of the dome, but the risk was great. Why, she wondered, shaking her hair free of the damp, adding a log to the fire, waiting for his return, why is the dome so important? It is true, came the answer. But why it should be so, she could not say. And why the voicing of truth should seem so necessary when imbalance and bereavement might follow? She could not say.

When, however, she told Tavis in the comforting darkness of their bed, after she realized on her second visit that she would need help in clambering up to clean the dome, it made no immediate difference. If he had known of it, he did not say; his love-making at dawn held the same quality of giving and withholding, the fierceness a result of her openness, not his. His tenderness later was perhaps greater, as though she were child more than woman. He carried the long ladder to the clearing, helped her scrub the mirrors with soft brushes dipped in tepid water, stretching out his arms to the very top where she could not reach, and rubbed the dome dry with a cloth while she held the ladder and rested.

They looked for a door or a window as they scrubbed and cleaned. Any mechanism that would gain them entrance, and she imagined that the distance between them was growing less. But it soon became clear that the dome was impenetrable. Though she had searched eagerly, she felt a curious relief, and was content to tackle the tall weeds with spade and fork, turning over the rich earth crawling with creatures, sowing seed of scented flowers where the ground had been cleared, and watching shoots spring up almost overnight.

But Tavis, as soon as he saw there was no means of entry, begrudged every minute spent at the dome. Ramyna saw his face harden with resentment and by late spring she realized her secret had been a source of closeness only while it remained a secret. Her speaking and even more Tavis' sharing the task of clearing and cleaning, had somehow driven him away. At dusk she saw that he no longer looked at her reflection in darkening windows, his evening silence stretched out through the night and into the day, any contact the clumsy search for relief. She had thought the danger lay in speaking, not in the dome itself. She knew his one determination was to find a way in, and wondered whether they could finally come close if she helped him, but recoiled at the thought. From indifference tinged with curiosity her reaction to penetrating the impenetrable had changed to revulsion and fear; she had been unable to keep this from him, as if the voicing of her one secret had opened a dam and she could keep nothing from him, while he remained closed and secretive. Their distance had been nothing compared to what it was now: she regretted her words, that had so altered him; only when tending it could she not regret the dome's existence and the effect it had had. The greater the danger of resentment growing, the more determinedly she set her steps towards the dome, and wondered that the cause of her pain should also be the source of comfort.

By the dome Ramyna could sometimes smile that what she would have thought trivial, the desire to enter the dome, not be content to look on it, was the cause of estrangement; only once, on a day when the forest was a rout of ferns and bluebells and the trees quivered with nests and birdsong, and she had gone to the dome as was now her daily habit, had walked around barefoot, so used to her reflection she no longer noticed it, but careful to see that the ground was clear of weed, that the glass shone in dazzling clarity, that the flowers were growing and spreading, scenting the air, and had sat a little way from it, basking in the warmth of reflections; only that day had she glimpsed, and been startled by the awareness, that she was to blame, that she had been the one to seek, by voicing her secret, to penetrate the impenetrable. Before she could lay hold of it, a cloud covered the sun, its shadow hid the reflection, and the thought was lost.

Soon she refrained from thinking of Tavis unless she was at the dome, where the pain of their estrangement was dulled by the blazing of two suns. In their forest home she gave her mind to the busy tasks of spring and summer, made herself content to minister to him, and went frequently to visit her family on the other side of

the forest, eager for news of Athon, and ready to help Thera pack
a growing collection of flowers that she was to take with her to the
new home where she would have more space to hang them.

*

One night Tavis walked around the dome in a dream, knowing
someone was inside. He heard a cry, echoed, when he woke with a
start, by Ramyna's restless sleep. He lay until she was quiet, then
rose and dressed, glancing briefly to make sure she still slept.
Quietly he closed the door and stepped into the forest, carrying a
spade and a lamp that swayed with each step. The clear crowded
sky seemed to draw closer as he neared the dome, making the lamp
unnecessary by the time he walked out into the clearing; the mirror
received the glimmer of stars and reflected it, casting a cool light
on the sleeping cattle, the carefully tended border where flowers
bowed their corollae and withheld scent from the night and as Tavis
approached it shone, mimicking his steps.

After circling the dome, searching, as if darkness might have
provided an entrance, he threw his spade in fury to shatter the
image, and made a crack like a spider's thread. But the dome,
caught unawares in its sleep, woke to defend itself and even the
third, violent throw cracked it no further: Tavis' face looked out at
him, distorted by anger and frustration. Trying to ignore it, he
trampled on the borders and began to dig, uprooting bulbs and
burying flowers under the moist earth.

When the sun rose and looked at itself in the mirrors, Tavis had
dug a moat a few yards long and lay resting. The glass was
embedded deep in rock, but Tavis did not believe it would be the
same all the way around. He continued to dig until he knew Ramyna
would be coming, then walked across to the opposite end from
where she would enter the clearing and into the forest. He slept in
dappled sunlight, woke, chilled at dusk and returned to the dome.

That night and the next he dug, until the dome stood at the
centre of a deep moat that laid bare solid rock foundations all
round. The dome was impregnable: even the thread markings had
healed by the third night. Defeated, Tavis returned to Ramyna and
entered her briefly and brutally before turning away into a heavy
sleep.

The following spring, as her family prepared to welcome Athon back from a voyage through scorched deserts, Ramyna gave birth to their son Nathar.

Athon brought them as a gift an irregularly shaped translucent stone with jagged points. In the light it revealed colours Ramyna and Tavis had never seen. and in shadow it shone as if it had its own light. Before he and Thera left in late summer, on a hot afternoon when only the breeze knew that autumn was on its way, as they walked through woods and sat by streams whose spring song had diminished to a murmur, Athon showed Tavis how the stone seemed to cut through the thickest glass like knife through bread. That night, for the first time since the winter Ramyna had revealed the secret of the dome to him, Tavis looked at her reflection in the windows and buried his hand in her dark hair as she nursed Nathar. Later he left them sleeping, Ramyna's breast still exposed to the suckling baby, and went into the forest, clutching the stone until it made welts in his hand.

3 Tavis' Story

It was dark when Tavis went to the dome. For a while he was guided by a light swaying high among the branches, as if a giant were walking ahead carrying a lamp. He imagined he heard the rustle of steps crushing leaves, but when he stood still to listen, the forest was silent save for the occasional crackle of trees settling into sleep. As soon as the light disappeared, he noticed a glimmer through the trees, like the anticipation of moonrise, that became brighter as he moved towards it. Suddenly he was in the clearing, looking on the dome which cast a pale light all around, reaching as far as the edge of the forest. He walked to the side where a strong beam from the wide open door streaked the grass; the vast circular hall was unfurnished, and a debris of wood and stone lay on the ground. Tavis stepped over it, kicking the occasional fragment away, puzzled by the emptiness. The dome was lit by a daylight, but the atmosphere was strange, as if he had come to a patch of cool desert.

—What am I doing here?—Tavis wondered, picking up a piece
of wood. He cradled it in his hand, enjoying the texture, the cavities
and deformities of a long process of decay, fingering it until a sense
of recognition passed from his hands up his spine: the form
reminded him of something, although he could not say what. He
turned it this way and that, lifted it high, held both pointed ends,
then the middle where the wood had shaped itself into a rounded
projection, and suddenly saw it:—it's like an eagle in flight—he
thought. And immediately the wood acquired the grace of the
winged creature he had occasionally seen hovering or diving to take
its prey. Eagerly he set down the eagle and picked up a fragment
of stone.—Will this be something too?—he wondered, handling the
rough object until it revealed the shape of an animal curled up in
sleep, that looked either like a cat or a mole.

In a few moments Tavis had a collection of creatures in wood
and stone. He sat on a stump, gathered the dozen or so animals to
him and handled now this now that, puzzled:—what am I doing
here?—he asked himself, looking through the glass at the landscape
beyond, resting his eyes on the green of grass and trees, following
the tranquil swish of the cows' tails and the rhythm of their chewing
as they grazed nearby. A couple of blackbirds flew up from a
branch; he thought he saw the antlers of a deer moving in the wood,
and peered into the shadows broken by sunrays. His eyes returned
to scan the emptiness of the moonscape around him, and he looked
again at the objects that hid shapes from the world outside. He
rose, walked, sat at the other end, walked again, picked up shapeless
fragments and tried to work out a form before casting them away.

—What am I doing here?—he asked himself finally, and walked
out into the night. Almost half-way across the clearing, darker now,
as if the light from the dome was fading, he remembered the eagle.
But the door was closed, and for many years Tavis forgot the dome,
although he experienced the sense of a dream recognized but not
remembered whenever he came upon strangely shaped pieces of
wood in the forest, or when he gathered large pebbles smoothed by
the water in the streams where he swam during summers.

*

One spring when he was a young man, Tavis met Thera and fell
in love. Her skin was like that of a pebble warmed by the sun, her

hair softer than the fur of any animal, her shape exciting to trace with his fingers and lips. He loved her until in autumn he thought:—she's not like anything—and returned to the clearing. The reflection of the sun on the glass made the whole area hot and dazzling, and the dome itself almost invisible. At first he half-closed his eyes against the glare, but got quickly used to the light and heat, recognized the dome he had visited a long time before, and remembered the eagle. He knew the door would be open: the interior had not changed, even the small pile of animal-like objects lay in wait for him where he had sat. What had changed was the light: Tavis saw that although the interior was lit by a daylight, when he looked out, he looked into night.—That's strange—he thought.— Does it mean anything?—

Near the stump of trunk he noticed a small knife with a decorative motif carved into the handle.—Was this here last time?—he wondered, intrigued that it might have been and he had not seen it. If it had not, however, how came it to be there now? He looked again and noticed, scattered among the wood and stone, various other tools: a scalpel, a hammer, a chisel, all with highly wrought decorations on the handles.—I see—he laughed, collecting the tools and sitting down. He shut his eyes, trying to remember the landscape he had seen the first time he had come. When the picture was recomposed in his mind, he realized that what was required of him was not merely to reproduce what he had seen, but to include what had been there but had remained unseen: he had seen no eagle, but an eagle had been flying through; he had seen no mole, but it too had been there, asleep underground.—I'll have to start by painting the background—he thought, deciding to find the material and return the next day. But the door was closed.—Why?—he wondered, trying to find the handle or some leverage to open it. He searched the ground nearby for a crowbar and noticed that what he had taken for the long trunk of a sapling was in fact a roll of canvas.—Nothing is what it seems, it would seem—he thought.—Twigs are really brushes, and leaves paint.—

—I wonder what I am?—he mused as he dragged the heavy canvas to the tree stump.—Not what I seem, it would seem—he concluded, gathering the tools. He sat back and shut his eyes to recompose the landscape of his childhood in order to reproduce it.

*

When Tavis finished the background he set to work on the stone
and wood: certain pieces seemed to contain the shape, all he had
to do was handle them for a minute and he knew which animal,
insect or plant it should be. Others were difficult. He spent many
hours feeling textures and forms, searching for a fragment of the
world he was trying to recreate; odd phrases would dart across his
mind, shear a donkey, flog a corpse, tie a dolphin by the tail, hold
an eel in a fig-leaf. He returned to the door, hoping it would be
open, that he could leave. But it remained firmly closed, and nothing
dented the glass except at the four points from which the tapestry
hung, where the nails had slipped in as if there had always been a
hole for them.

Almost invariably though, the pieces eventually yielded themselves to him, and Tavis could add some object to the landscape
he was making until at last only ten of the largest blocks eluded
him; half a dozen stone blocks and three sections of tree-trunk, all
roughly the same size; and the only marble block, that loomed high
above the rest, its top almost touching the ceiling of the dome. He
sat, surrounded by creatures and plants, looking out to a large
clearing crossed by paths through cropped grass which curved
around the dome from all directions, intersecting four or five times
within yards of it. At the far end, near the forest, were small herds
of animals, horses, stags, cows, grazing peacefully. The whole scene
was brilliantly lit.

—It doesn't look like what I saw—Tavis thought—the green of
the grass has too much yellow in it, the leaves have too much grey
and the sky not enough; the tree-trunks are too red to be brown;
and the animals . . . He walked around, rearranging, hiding this
insect, burying deeper that underground animal, trying to give a
greater sense of flight by changing the angle at which the two
blackbirds were perched on the end of a long twig he had pared
down to thread-like slenderness.—It doesn't look real—he thought.
He tried the door again, hoping he could go now that the moonscape
had been altered to bear some resemblance to the world beyond,
but it was still closed, and Tavis returned to circle the pieces he
had been unable to fashion.

—Something's missing—he concluded some time later.—I must
introduce what is not there in order to go free—he thought.

—What?—I don't know—he realized, sitting on a stump and shutting his eyes: Ramyna came towards him on the grass outside the dome. The outline of her body was clearly defined by the material that covered it, her breasts trembled, her shoulders appeared where the gown had slipped, and her bare legs through long splits that opened with her stride. She looked at him without smiling and Tavis opened his eyes abruptly. When he saw she was not in fact walking towards him he shut his eyes again just in time to see her disappear. The gown left the whole back bare, the buttocks swayed with each step. When she'd gone, Tavis replayed the gesture of sliding his hand around to the breast, pulling the gown off to feel the texture of her skin, the shape of her belly. He was shaking.—Her?—he wondered, when the trembling had subsided a little.—Yes—he realized, standing in front of the blocks.

He set to work on the wood: the trunks were different, and Tavis began by working on the section of ash, moulding it into a tall graceful figure striding towards the canvas landscape. The wood was like clay: it shaped itself into material and the curves of a body in firm and confident lines. As he chiselled Tavis was aware of the complete familiarity of the body: though clothed, it was a body he had seen and known naked, whose every fold his hands knew as he knew every line on his hands. Yet he had never seen Ramyna before: he did not know how he knew her name was Ramyna. It wasn't until he attempted to fashion the face that he realized the figure emerging from the wood was nothing like the woman that had come in a vision: when he tried to recapture the roundness of cheek and lip, the fairness of skin and hair, the scalpel slipped into shaping high prominent cheekbones, large almond-shaped eyes, a frame of dark, coarse, unruly hair, a face without softness though not lacking tenderness. And when he stood back and realized he had in front of him a wooden statue of Thera, he threw the scalpel across the hall in anger and strode towards the door.—Enough of this—he thought, tugging at the door. It yielded immediately, opening out on to the clearing that was bathed in the pink light of sunset. A gust stroked his face once, and was quiet. Nothing moved. Tavis was about to take a step out when he thought:—what have I been doing?—and looked back at the world he had made. The hall was full of merely objects. A figure he knew but could not recognize as Thera stood stiff, empty-eyed; shapes that could, but need not, be birds or animals were scattered, a large canvas splashed with greens and yellows hung precariously on nails in front of a segment mirror, the marble block loomed above everything like a faceless giant, and the stone and wood stood without meaning or shape.

—I must find Thera: she's not like anything.—Tavis thought. He closed the door and began to walk away from the clearing, stroking, as he passed them, the thick flanks of the pasturing cows, and picking from the cropped grass the occasional buttercup. Neither resembled the texture of anything that he had fashioned inside the dome: the hide was coarser, but warmer; the flowers fragile and elastic. Then he saw two figures approach the dome from different directions. One was tall, graceful, beautiful, the other was real. Tavis looked with angry yearning at the one, but stepped with determination towards the other, and when he held Thera's hand, whose texture resembled nothing—like is not real—he told her. He knew he was free when she leant towards him and touched his lips with hers.—Real is like nothing—she told him.

4 Ramyna's Grief

Ramyna was woken by Nathar's whimpering and knew Tavis had gone: she had known in her sleep, feeling without need to be awake the emptiness of the bed through a dream in which she was Athon trudging through deserts where sand swirled in her face and heat created mirages of woods and streams that retreated as she approached, but always in sight so as not to crush her hope of relief from the sun. In the dream she had glimpsed through the trees the top of the dome, framed in light.

She lay until hunger turned Nathar's whimper into a yell, slowing her heartbeat to quietness, shrouding herself in will. Since the summer Tavis left her for three nights to dig the moat that destroyed the flower-bed, Ramyna had known he would go and prepared herself for it. Even when she realized she had conceived, and knowledge was pushed back behind hope that the child would restore the closeness the dome had destroyed, she continued to close herself from him, puzzling at the same time that she should be, slowly and painfully, closing when she knew hope lay in openness. The longer Tavis stayed, the more firmly she hoped and the more firmly she subverted it by closing herself from him, concentrating her attention on the birth and the puckered red-faced creature whose features soon smoothed into babyhood, whose eyes opened and followed her movements, entranced by her reflection as it danced in and out of the lamplight against the black windows.

Now he had gone, she thought, and drew Nathar to her, covered him in the blanket and lay back on the pillows as he suckled. But how necessary is hope to the will: while Ramyna packed her belongings and arranged for the furniture to be stored that she could not take with her to the child's room across the forest, she observed herself hoping, and wondered at the stubbornness of the self still prepared to imagine that Tavis would walk in from the rain that crashed to earth undaunted all through the following weeks, bringing with it the penetrating damp of autumn. Hope, she thought once, taking crockery from the tall kitchen cupboard and packing it between straw in wooden boxes, was like the dome: she knew it was empty. Yet the illusion it created of possibilities that could be realized was somehow necessary precisely to confront its emptiness. The thought, difficult to formulate and to retain, slipped into others and was hidden, but hope remained.

She considered going to the dome, as if her hope would be better realized there, but found chores filled her time too fully: where would she leave Nathar? Once she was back, she argued, she could leave the child with her mother, one of her sisters. Then she would go. She did not allow the awareness that she was missing the one opportunity to become thought, and never became conscious that there was nothing to prevent her from taking Nathar with her. Instead she indulged in fantasies of Tavis' return, seeing his face in the windows, looking in on her from the outside; glimpsing his back as he vanished into the undergrowth while she picked the last sodden vegetables; mistaking any man whose features bore some resemblance to Tavis and following him through the village. Rocking the child to sleep, she replayed day after day the identical sequence of his return: the sound of his feet stamping mud and water from his boots, shaking his coat of rain; pushing back wet hair from his forehead—droplets remained on his beard and dried as he stood in front of the fire, rubbing his hands until they were warm; he came across, traced the delicate features of the child with his fingers, buried his other hand in her dark hair.

Before the first snows, however, Ramyna had moved across the forest. The home she had shared with Tavis was bolted and locked and soon buried under a white tarpaulin. Once she was away from the house, Ramyna was free of hope; a pain took its place that left her tossing in vain search of relief throughout the nights. Why, why, why. There was no answer, except the dome: she saw it, smothered in weeds that grew and covered it, filthy with bird excrement, impregnable and mysterious, drawing her to itself, a source of truth and the cause of lie, source of hope and cause of pain; the cause of pain and the source of comfort. But she rejected it and would not go.

During the day she was cheerful. She helped her mother in her tasks, went with her father to attend to forest duties, played with Nathar, rejoiced when the occasional message arrived from Thera, inevitably accompanied by either a drawing or an example of some rare flower she had found, and, like a child, joined her brothers and sisters in their games. It was as if the day raised a wall against the pain and she could, at moments, look at her night mourning as on that of a stranger and be puzzled by it. At night she knew what a consummate torturer she was, that daytime relief was simply a way to make the night freshly painful. She almost forgot Nathar at night, rising automatically to answer his cries without annoyance and without tenderness, weaving still the tapestry that daylight would undo, leaving threads ready for the next night.

Day was punctuated by change: while winter melted into spring, spring hardened into summer, summer dissembled into autumn, Nathar's eyes became bright with the pleasure of movement and the beginning of speech, hours filled with the sounds of ecstasies and terrible tears. Ramyna looked on him as an extension of herself, a particularly vital limb that needed special care but was not separate; when he became tangled in his uncertain legs as he raced among the trees, through paths crackling with red, brown and yellow leaves, it was as if she had stumbled and fallen, and the comfort of her embrace was the same consolation she would have proffered to herself. He ceased crying almost immediately, distracted by the least thing from the boredom of tears. She knew him precisely as she knew herself, there was no difference, she thought as he slept; and did not see the contradiction between his sleep and her wakefulness.

Night was timeless, she thought, unwilling to acknowledge its changes. But in fact grief hollowed into a vacuum that grew increasingly arid until there was no emotion and no possibility of knowing and expressing feeling. As Nathar's eyes brightened, hers dulled: Athon told her how shocked he was by the change in her. She was jolted into something that resembled life by his return the following year in the month of deepest winter, hope of hope flickered momentarily and was extinguished when he left at the height of spring, telling her she should come with him, away from the forest, to look on different worlds. During that summer, a particularly hot season that withered leaves before time and burnt ferns, Ramyna insistently asked herself whether she was not herself the cause of her emptiness: had she not made Tavis go by revealing a secret best kept a secret? Had she not wanted him to go, somehow? Was she not indulging in an unreal mourning? When she had run in the track of this thought, she returned full circle and spun, deepening the rut with each lap.

Once during that time she found herself at the dome and looked into the mirror: the image cast back was perfect, but empty, flattened by impregnable surface. Behind it was blackness. Yet the word behind was not right, it implied depth, and if there was no depth in the image, neither was there in the surface through which it came. There was merely the illusion of depth. Ramyna wondered whether the dome was not only empty—she had known that since Tavis left—but itself illusion, and walked around to make sure it filled space; though when she had measured the steps and the time it took to circle it, she was not reassured: was the fact of space a guarantee of reality? It was as if the recognition of her own emptiness, reflected in the surfaceless image that came back from the mirror cast doubt on the existence of space and therefore the reality that her ability to circle the dome implied. Was not the dome merely a convex reflection of the image? Were not emptiness and image as much synonyms as existence and reality? Why, she asked herself, why should it be that darkened glass became an object empowered with reflections, to cast back images that gave the illusion of reality? Why?

She saw that the mirror received and cast back her image with total indifference, that it made no difference to the smooth glass if she was there; that once she was out of reach of its power to reflect, she no longer had any existence. Her daily life, because outside the sphere of what mirrors could reflect, was not real. Her suffering was not real because the dome did not show it. All it showed was a barefoot woman in a mauve and purple sari, looking at herself. Analysis and description of each feature, the thin arched eyebrows, the straight nose, the high cheekbones, the dark, widely separated eyes, the carefully shaped mouth, the unruly black hair, made no difference. She remained surface.

*

One hot day in early autumn, Ramyna, Nathar and her younger brothers and sisters retreated deep into the forest in search of moist undergrowth and refreshing stream. Ramyna walked and the children bounded past places where she and Tavis had stripped and lain long before, and Ramyna examined the staked indifference that kept her rigid and on guard, and was irked by the tedium of grief. Why take it so hard? She wondered, watching her child's exhilaration at everything he encountered. Tavis had taken all joy with him, she thought, and she abruptly resented it with an intensity and anger that raced up her spine and vanished.

When they reached the widening in the bed of the stream called the pool they dived into the shallow water. Nathar squealed his delight as his older companions showered him and pushed him gleefully into the water: he fought them with vigour, unaware of their gentleness.

Ramyna sat on a rock in the shade and watched them. Trees on either side of the stream embraced, forming an arch through which the occasional rays penetrated, playing on the wet skin of the children. The clear water whirled, muddied by the crashing of their games. Blue and green dragonflies darted past: Ramyna remembered how Tavis had told her dragonflies lived for only three days. She had not wondered then why this should be, she had accepted that fact as completely as she had accepted his love and her love for him, as completely as she had accepted the child when he arrived after his love had died. Only now could she lie with her eyes half-closed, listening to the yells of the children and question it. Was it necessary that dragonflies should exist for three days only? Had it been necessary for their love to exist at all if it was going to die after three days? Was her tedious mourning simply the refusal to accept an inevitable death, death inevitable? So pointless, she thought, opening her eyes; the children had gone quiet, except for sharp bursts of laughter. They lay on rocks, leaning over the water that had darkened with mud and become mirror. They were playing at making faces, distorting their features into monstrous creatures with the help of fingers and tongues, and displaying their master-pieces to each other's peals of laughter. Nathar, too young to know fully the coordination of hands, lips and eyes required, tried and stared with an amazement that prevented him from laughing with the others. As she looked at him, Ramyna suddenly saw him trapped inside mirrors, running from one side of the dome to the other, beating his fist against the smooth walls, his lips shaped into a shout she could not hear. No, she thought, shutting her eyes against the vision, not Nathar, he is me, he is not separate, he is not unknown. But she could hardly touch the child, afraid of the passion in her embrace when he clambered, wet, into her arms, leant against her chest and stuck two fingers in his mouth, still watching the older ones, tireless in their games. Her heart beat so fast and loudly with love and terror that Nathar lifted his bewildered head. Ramyna stretched her lips into a smile and stroked his hair. Comforted the child lay back. She rocked him, quietening the hammering, until he had fallen asleep, then laid him on the rock, his clothes a pillow, her dress a blanket.

She would lose him, she thought, trudging back while the day, exhausted by heat, waited for relief of setting sun and evening breeze. Nathar was asleep still, hoisted on her shoulders. Ramyna's breath came short and drops of sweat slid down her face, down her belly, down her thighs. It was not only the heat, soon he would be too heavy to carry. She sat on a trunk, faint with an anguish that eclipsed anything she had experienced in her loss of Tavis. She would lose him, she would lose him, and she could not close herself from him. It became a beat, insistent and useless, as evidence of her child's separateness accumulated. She asked him, one day as they gathered kindling wood, what are you thinking? Nothing, he said, and the vision of the dome rose sharp and clear. Inevitably, with self-destructive insistence, she analysed the quality of the new pain that had so swiftly overwhelmed the old frayed mourning over a man she had never really loved. Not as she loved the child, she added quickly to justify the betrayal, and uncertain even as she formed the thought, as to what she meant by love: was it not like the dome, a series of reflecting mirrors in which we seek others to find only ourselves and seek ourselves to be shocked into the discovery of the strangeness of another? Where the loss of Tavis had left her acquiescent and listless, the fear and knowledge of the inevitable separation from Nathar left her floundering, panic-stricken. She was in the dome, she thought, pacing her mind like a caged animal, she must escape. How to escape loss? How to escape from fear of loss?

She would not lose him, she realized finally, triumphantly, the following summer, waiting for her twin's return; she would leave him. And was immediately lifted out of the cage she had paced for a year: she would leave him not to lose him. How absurd, she thought. Why? How could it be that by leaving her son she would not lose him? Was it not true that she had already lost him, that she had never had him except when he had been bound to her in her belly? Had not the first kick heralded their separation and his first cry her loss of him? How could it be that by leaving she would not lose him? There was no reason to it. But the dome was neither the creator nor a creation of reason.

5 Ramyna's Journeys

—Where shall I begin?—she asked Athon.

—From here of course—he answered, pointing with a sweep of his arm to the sea.

—Where shall I go then?—she asked smiling. The sun was on her face and reflection from the water lit her eyes.

—Everywhere.—He laughed too.

—Everywhere? That is too vast, isn't it?—she answered.

—Yes, but not impossible.—

—Help me choose.—

Athon rose and helped her to her feet: they had been sitting on sand so fine it had the texture of petals.

—It's not a question of choice. But let's toss for it.—He picked up a slate-coloured stone.

—If it falls where the groove is, come with me. If not, go in the opposite direction.—

—Alone?—

—Why not?—

—I don't want to be alone.—

—You don't think you won't be alone with me, do you?—

Ramyna looked up at him. Athon smiled, then turned to the sea, frowning the pale lines around the eyes and lips into creases against the glare. He knows the dome, she thought. Like her, he was trying to escape it. Or maybe not. She was startled by the thought: what had it to do with where they, she, went and how and why? Whether she was alone or not? And anyway, she knew he must know the dome. Hadn't he described it when they were children, put into words what to her had merely been an awareness? But it could have been a dream. She shook sand from her dress and moved towards the group of houses behind them. Athon tossed the stone in the air, then skimmed it to the water so that it bounced once before sinking.

—Go on the sea.—He said as he caught up with her.

—All right.—

—It is the strangest.—

—Do I want anything strange?—She turned to him: the desire to speak of the dome stopped her in her tracks.

—Don't you?—Athon didn't look at her and kept walking.

—I don't know what I want.—

—Is it a question of want?—

—What else?—

—I don't know.—He turned and looked out at the sea again, then grinned.

—The sea then.—

—The sea.—

So she was alone, she thought, leaning over the rails and looking
out at the blue-green desert: foam splintered the water in the middle
distance. Further, sea and sky met in identical planes. Immediately
above her seagulls cut into the blue, diving to the water and
hovering above the mast. The sun was warm on her back, cold
wind blew her black hair in a tangle of curls and spray stiffened
her cheeks. They were equally distant from any shore, safe from all
land, Ramyna thought. Safe from Nathar? Safe from Tavis? Safe
from grief and loss? Safe from the dome. She knew that was illusion:
her mind was a hill at the base of which a single ditch had been
dug—a single ditch had always been there—and all thought, like
water, found its way to it and deepened it. She had to dig another
ditch, redirect some of the water or nothing would grow. What
strange images, she thought. Why think in terms of growing?
Growing to what? The ditch was somehow connected with the
dome. And dome and ditch were the same, just images. Images of
what, though? Image is everywhere, Ramyna concluded, catching
sight of her shadow on the water. Another shadow joined it, and
Ramyna smiled at the fellow-traveller who leant over the rails next
to her. Pray, release from thought, she thought as they walked the
length and breadth of the ship, explored the area below, ended up
late one night on deck in a bed of rope and made a new love filled
with the smell of engine and the taste of salt.

He had an unimportant name and a handsome face: when she
began her travels of mountains she wondered that his name should
have been so unimportant, that she could have so easily forgotten
his face. Why then had they met and explored the sea together?
Had they come together merely to explore the sea together? She
had not wanted to be alone. Had she been less alone with him? He
called the love-making by terms that were more apt, she thought,
remembering the violence with which Tavis had entered her when
she had conceived Nathar: one-syllable words with hard sounds that
reflected exactly what they did and the harshness of the pleasure. He
called a spade a spade, he told her. Yet she could not bring herself
to use the words: some necessity of tenderness required her to soften
them, though she could see clearly the absurdity. In what way
could they be said to be making love? Didn't making imply some
durability, some permanence of what is made? Had even Tavis and

she made anything except a child? And a child is durable and permanent, she thought. But he is not love, he is loss.

They were careful not to burden themselves with children when they abandoned ship and set up house close to the beach from where they could travel far out to sea, to fish and contend with changeable winds and sudden storms.

—Thera returned with her daughter when mother died.—Athon told her when they met at the foot of jagged mountains.

—She has a daughter?—Ramyna said.

—Yes, also called Thera. The father insisted . . .

—The father?—

—I don't know. She is caring for Nathar.—

She had not heard the name of her child spoken out loud for too long. A blush spread like light. Her hands were sweating and she was not sure whether her heart had stopped or was beating faster. Could she bring out his name?

—Shall I go home?—she asked him. Athon rose and took a few steps away from her.

—Do you want to?—

—I want Nathar.—The name cut her tongue.

—Thera is caring for him.—

—Yes, of course.—Ramyna mumbled. So he was lost to her. She had left him not to lose him, but he was lost. She had not thought of him, merely carried him inside her, too precious to bring into the light.

—Where shall I go now?—she asked him gaily, not looking at him.

—To the top, why not?—he replied, pointing to the rocky crest of a nearby mountain covered in snow.

—Will you come with me?—she tried to keep the plea from her question.

—You are better alone.—

And for a long time Ramyna climbed alone: mountains were simpler than the sea, she realized. The contest with the sea was against what had no stillness, no permanence. Each storm required a new knowledge, that could only be acquired during the storm and became useless and sometimes increased the danger in tackling the next. The only security was the boat, and the boat was at the mercy of the sea. Each time she and her lover had been in a storm they had confronted the possibility of death, and the shared elation when they docked in the small bay and threw themselves exhausted on the sand was the elation of the gambler who stakes all and wins; the elation drove them to gamble again, in a cycle that had no purpose apart from the elation of repeating the gamble until the inevitable defeat. The contest with mountains was no gamble, because the mountains did not change. Once she had learnt the formation of the rock, the distance between one step and the next, all the contest required was the habit of skill: as long as she did not allow her foot to slip or attention to be distracted by the wind tearing at her face, she was safe, and the elation when she reached a peak was the elation of achievement. The only danger was in looking down. The first time she had wanted to measure the distance and looked below into the crag she had swayed in the terror of vertigo and almost lost her foothold on the narrow icy projection.

*

—Don't be so serious—the lover from the mountains told her soon after they met in a refuge crowded with men, women and children drinking and laughing.

—Don't look at me—he warned as they set out on their first climb.

—Keep your eyes on the mountain.—

—I don't know—he answered when she asked him why they climbed, why they were lovers, why the dome existed, what the dome was, had he seen it.—Stop thinking—he laughed at her—and stop asking questions. And don't ask me why we should laugh: I don't know.—

She was transformed into unthinking, laughing, until her lover's foot slipped one clear icy afternoon and she watched him drop, creating an upheaval of snow-dust where he bounced like a rubber doll against the rocks. She could have let herself fall too, she thought later. Why hadn't she? Why was it not finished yet? she wondered as she prepared to leave the mountains and journey home. They had stood side by side against the rock face, not looking at each other, gripping with calloused hands at projections, measuring the distance for the next step; on their return from climbing to the top of mountains they had sat side by side in refuges crowded with drinking laughing people and been, in love; she had talked of the dome so casually it had ceased for a while to be mystery, she thought on the caravan that was taking her across deserts to the sea. They had not looked at each other: she had been loved though she had not been known, she had loved and not sought to know. But as she boarded the ship she realized that the lover from the mountains was becoming, perhaps had always been, a way to knowledge. Through him she understood how men and women loved, without thought, how only the unreflecting could be, in love; how knowledge was the destroyer of love. She recognized, as the winter sea rocked the ship in its leaden arms, that now she was barred from love by knowledge. Knowledge could never be unknown, it merely fed on experience until it became a giant that swallowed the simple wish to be. And as to be and to love were synonymous, because she could not be, neither could she love. The realization stilled her from all restlessness, so that it was at the moment of profoundest knowledge of the impossibility of loving, while the stone-coloured sky released a volley of sharp rain, that she was closest to being.

The sky cleared, the sea dipped itself in blue and the ship drew near to land. When Ramyna recognized, in the tall man waving at her from the shore, her son Nathar, she was stilled further by the realization that if the love that could exist between a man and a woman eluded her, she did after all love; and because she had left him, because she had held her child without thought after she had left him, her love was unchanged. She would have to engage in every subterfuge to refrain from seeking knowledge if she was to survive in her son's love, and he in hers. Thought was the agent of knowledge, the agent of change and loss. She would have to be wily to subvert its power and hold the love for her son to protect it from death. As she thought she wondered whether the thought was already damaging the love, and carefully, with absolute determination, she laid it aside, and when she greeted her tall son and his wife, Thera, she was able to be, in love, with them.

Soon after she returned to the forest and joined her son's household, Ramyna sought the dome, with the strange certainty that it was required of her that she should go. She walked along the familiar paths: at one point the forest would cease to be known and she would be on her way to the dome. She pictured it as she had first seen it, hoping that the picturing would somehow translate her into that first time. But the memory of the last time she had found herself there superimposed itself with insistence. She had looked at mirrors and seen herself, she had not looked further to what the mirrors protected, the dome itself. She had lost Tavis because he had been unable to accept the dome's refusal to allow him to penetrate it, and she had blamed him, his stubborn determination, his inability to accept surfaces and be content. But had she not been equally to blame, more to blame for revealing the existence of the dome to him? She had wanted to know him as he had sought to penetrate the dome, there too there were reflections. Oh, she regretted her inability, her culpable inability to understand that she could not know: she had not known Tavis, she had not known her nameless lover and would never know Nathar. Was she still searching, as she was now searching for the dome? The dome was becoming in her mind like the stone she remembered Athon bringing back, the stone Tavis took with him. So many sides and lights apparently coming from within and reflected from without, so many contradictory truths—ah, but the word truth was inadequate, it limited the dome. She was glad she was going and would no longer have to think of it, make words for whatever it was and meant.

Ramyna looked around: the setting sun came obliquely through the trees, rising mist veiled the undergrowth, damp air penetrated through the shawls and wet ground chilled her feet; the path was familiar and though she walked on, closing her attention to the direction, it was still familiar when long shadows had taken over from light and the cold made it difficult for her to move with ease. She stood, blowing to warm her hands, and watched her breath merge with the thickening fog. She had walked in the large circle she remembered best from childhood, when she had not known the forest and had been startled to find herself on the way home, just at the moment when she was about to moan her tiredness and demand that her father carry her. The dome eluded her. She could not find it—but find was not the right word, it had never been a question of seeking, she had always known when she should go, though she had sometimes refused to. Must she now seek it? she wondered heading back to the edge of the forest.

6 A Lover's Story

The room had been carefully chosen to suit her. It was large, at least twenty feet by thirty, and spacious: the ceiling so high that without spectacles I could not distinguish the shell-shaped mould-ings decorating it. The longer northern wall was taken up almost completely by a tall glass door that opened outwards into a brick enclosure covered in virginia creeper and morning glory, about the same size as the room, and to a riot of flowers: daisies, speedwells, buttercups carpeted the lawn, in the centre of which stood a moun-tain ash; snowdrops, crocuses, primroses, lilies-of-the-valley, prim-ulas, and violets in the cool shade of the border under large ferns uncurling; daffodils, bluebells and cyclamen among the bracken and hart's-tongue, interrupted by mimosa and a fully grown plane tree in the corners of the north-facing wall, against the room; magnolia, lilac and hibiscus shrubs permanently in flower; hyacinths and narcissi, roses and sweet peas, lilies and pinks scented the air.

The evening I took her to the room, she barely looked at it in her eagerness to see the garden, and strode across it as the strongest rays of the setting sun dazzled the panes of the open glass door; for a second I was blinded and took off my spectacles to rub my eyes. When I opened them she was looking at me and stooped to kiss me with her mocking tenderness for my short-sightedness and awkward mien.

The reflection on the glass threw a rich gold-red light, and when-ever the breeze moved the leaves of the plane tree it shimmered around the room as we sat in comfortable armchairs aligned to the southern wall, with a brass standard lamp between, and examined its sparse furnishings: a king-size bed flanked by rosewood cabinets against the western wall; opposite, next to the door, a round table with two upright chairs in the same rosewood. The uncarpeted floor

was a parquet in interlacing patterns of a geometric motif; she told
me later that she could be absorbed for hours in working out the
relation between one shape and another. All the lampshades were
in a magnolia-coloured cotton cambric fringed with the same coral
muslin as the curtains I drew and the bedspread I watched her fold
back: the bare windowless walls had been painted a white mixed
with red that enhanced still more the glow when we switched on
the lights before I left, as if the room were the inside of a shell.

I returned to him aware of her moving around, her many shadows
intersecting on the floor, her tranquillity deepening the quiet of the
night; the definite movement of her wrist as she switched off the
standard lamp and the light on the table, the slight sinking of the
mattress when she sat on the edge of the bed, the rustle of sheets
as she slid under them and the sigh of darkness as the last light
was turned off and she slept.

He would be pleased.

Nothing happened for a time so long that its days and nights lose
any meaning and it is pointless to try and remember how many
years passed, how many decades, centuries. Only once during that
time did I witness their meeting. I sat in one of the upright chairs
with my elbows on the table, my chin in my hand, and watched
my beloved and his beloved walk the garden arm in arm in the cool
of the day, talking. She stooped above a red camellia and took the
calix in her hand, he drew near the narcissi and inhaled deeply;
they stood poised under the plane tree watching the top branches
still sparkling leaves, sat in silence in the leather armchairs to watch
the play of lights, discussed, before drawing the curtains, the stars
as they needle-pointed the sky. He went to her every evening just
as the sunset blazed and the day's morning glory bowed and folded
its petals, left when night was established: his hands cupped her
cheeks and he kissed her on the forehead before going.

He called for me when the shadows lengthened in the afternoon
and explained:—while I'm absent, I wish you to take my place;
look after her, go to her, stay with her through the gathering dusk,
walk with her, talk with her. Explain to her that I am called away.
I know she likes you—he smiled and patted the bald patch on the

crown of my head—and you like her. Go now, the sun is sinking, do not be late.—

I walked around the big irregularly constructed cloister, whose facing archways supported on slender columns were staggered so that instead of square it was rhomboid in shape. I took off my spectacles to lighten the burden of loss; my footsteps echoed. In an archway above the door was a fresco whose every detail I knew though I could not see it now: my eyes paused on a patch of brown that was a beautifully rendered stag, before I stepped out and let the door swing shut behind me.

*

In the morning she woke to the strange sound of pebbles being hurled to the ground outside the open glass door, the sight of drawn curtains tossing and fluttering wildly, and to an unfamiliar sensation: the hairs on her arms stood upright, her teeth knocked against each other uncontrollably, spasms went through her. She was cold. She had not been cold since she had come, nor had she been troubled by anything stronger than an evening breeze; rain had been an invisible, noiseless nightfall that washed clean the leaves and enriched still more the scents of the earth. Now she stepped in a pool of water and shut the glass, drew back the curtains to gaze at the lead-coloured sky dropping hail; the trees and the shrubs pitched in the wind, the lawn was covered with marbles, the garden transformed into a battlefield.

At sunset she was pacing the room in her long stride, clasping and unclasping her hands, her light hair pulled back in a tight bun.

The hail had settled into rain that lasted all day, and the sky was darkening without the usual celebration of colours. I brought blankets and a heater with me, and we huddled in the chairs: the light we switched on and the drawn curtains warmed the room, but the wet-powder smell had already stolen into the walls and floor.

We spoke of the extraordinary change, linked it to his absence and wondered how long it would be before he returned.

All her quietness had gone, and was only precariously restored by the time I left, strangely elated; she had clutched my hand in panic for a second, not wanting me to go. I reassured her she would wake in the morning to a blaze made all the greater by the uncharacteristic downpour and calmed her by reminding her of the flowers she was expecting to see open; but the kiss she gave me was troubled and humourless.

*

It continued to rain, it pitter-pattered and sighed, it crashed and wept until the garden was a mudfield. I came one evening to see her on her haunches in the incessant rain, keening in front of the last stalwart rose bush that had refused to flower; led her shivering back to the comparative warmth of the high-ceilinged room and spent my first night with her: she clung to me, dry-eyed, and I could not leave her. We crouched in a corner of the large bed, trying to fit our limbs to each other, as in a live jigsaw puzzle. But she and I did not belong to the same jigsaw, were not even cut out by the same hand; yet there was comfort in the warmth of the shared bed. And for me there was again the triumph of her need, which seemed to increase during the next seven years until I was certain nothing could reverse it, not even his return.

She was clasping and unclasping her hands when I came in one evening.

—Look—she said, and took my hand to show me. On the floor in the corner facing the door, next to the bed, was a large stain that extended up the wall; the paint flaked off in my hand, and the parquet sighed under my weight.

—It's the damp—I said.

—Yes—she said; she closed fingers over thumbs.

—There's none on the other side—I said walking around.

—I know, I looked—she said, following me a step behind.

—Anyway, it hasn't rained today—I said cheerfully. I switched on the standard lamp and sat down.

—No—she said. She looked down at me before turning to pace the room, twisting her fingers; she drew back the curtains: night was falling, grey merging into black. Apart from the darker shadow of the wall, very little could be seen of the garden, but she stood, shifting her weight from one foot to the other until the darkness was complete and she could see her outline, black against the window-panes.

—What this place needs is brightening up—she said as she drew the curtains across . . .

We camped with the furniture arranged in a defending circle around
the bed, used the table for pasting, chairs for ladders and glued on
to the walls wide strips of paper showing large red and orange
flower patterns and leaves of varied green that corresponded to
none we knew from the garden: it was as if they had been altered
by a distorting mirror or drawn from innacurate memory. But when
the damp patch was hidden and every inch covered with them, she
turned to me her old mocking smile and for a while her hands were
still as she rearranged the furniture, putting bed and cabinets where
the armchairs had been, the table in the middle of the room and
all chairs and the standard lamp in its place. The western side she
left bare . . .

Until I came back to find the floor covered and the room warmed
by a thick green carpet splashed with bright shapes in yellow,
blue and white; and the next evening damask curtains with grass-
coloured flowers across the glass and the door. The new bedspread
was a light-blue cotton print. She rearranged the furniture, huddling
chairs in the north-western corner and the table against the western
wall. The room was disturbing in the riot of its clashing patterns,
but it seemed to quieten her . . .

Though not for long: one evening I found her standing at an easel,
her cheeks and hands spattered with paint. She turned to me,
waving the paint brush, and said:
　—What this place needs is pictures: make it more human.—And
she showed me the first two paintings, roughly executed miniatures,
no bigger than four inches by two, one of violets in a vase, the other
a single flesh-coloured orchid almost obscene in the openness of
detail and the depth of observation.
　I returned each night to find a new painting of flowers drying on
the easel. Quite soon she began to paint objects, shells, glasses,
bottles, jars, plates, fruits, foods; then landscapes, interiors,
seascapes, city-scapes, depicted in a variety of styles: some strong-
coloured and in clearly delineated outlines, others in soft pastels
with edges blurred by light and shadow; some done with large bold
strokes and thick paint, others almost photographic in their flatness;
some were recognizable as object or scape, others were more or less

abstract shapes and geometric constructions. She had no favourite styles or theme—she seemed simply to want to pack the garish walls—though a recurrent motif was of objects reflected in mirrors, mountains in lakes, interiors in the play of glass, trees in ponds, the sun in the sea, paintings in empty studios, the moon on water.

While the walls were being hung and the room closed in a little further, the frown on her forehead disappeared and the mocking smile reappeared to greet me as I came in on cold wet evenings. I saw, as we sat and she paused in her contemplation now of one now of another of the pictures, that she wished I would not stay and share her bed; but she did not dare say it, fearful of her need and the recurring desolation of the rain beyond curtains that, though permanently drawn, failed to keep us from the hunching of shoulders against the chill.

—Describe me—she asked, and I told her about her height, her slenderness, her stride, the large hands and mouth, the eyes and blond hair, the definite movement of the wrist as she switched off the lights, the sinking of the mattress when she sat on the edge of the bed, the rustle of sheets as she slid under them.

—Describe me—she begged, and as I spoke of her mocking smile, the frown on her forehead, the paint on her cheek, she sketched her hands and feet and attached to them the figure of a gaunt dark-haired woman with marble-sized eyes . . .

A while later I noticed a damp patch spreading across the ceiling above the glass door; I saw it from the bed and though I knew, from the twisting of her hands, that she also had seen it, we did not discuss it. Instead, we talked of the portrait of me she wanted to paint. I sat in the armchair, with the standard lamp blanketing me in light; and she sketched me from all angles, from the remotest corner of the room as well as from the nearest point before the pose disintegrates into detail, but transformed me at her easel into a grey rock whose only recognizable feature was the glitter of glasses. She did not finish or hang it, though she rearranged the furniture for the last time, putting the bed diagonally across the north-western corner, table and chairs in the north-eastern corner and the armchairs in between, facing into the room . . .

Finally she brought three six-foot mirrors, displaced paintings and
fitted two facing each other on the side walls and one in the middle
of the southern wall. She stood in the centre of the room to see
herself from three angles; she stood in front of either side one to see
her back and a further reflection of her face, thrown to the facing
mirror from the one in front of which she was standing; she walked
around, found where she could not see herself and fitted a triptych
of narrow mirrors in the north-western corner. Wherever she stood
facing the room now she could see a full reflection of herself and
fragments of that reflection refracted on all the other mirrors. If she
stood with her back to the room, she still knew she could not escape
being caught in reflections, and spent the last evenings pacing or
sitting in an armchair absorbed in the intricate and unchanging
patterns: lamplights looking at each other across and through all
the mirrors, shadows intersecting at extraordinary angles; furniture,
paintings, us, the easel where the twelve by six canvas on which
she was working stood covered by a cloth, all endlessly repeated.

*

The dawn chorus was the clash of variously pitched instruments;
she drew back the curtains to a dazzle of light and gave me the
kiss, cupping her hands around my face, smiling . . .

. . . and in the evening the sunset blazed against the glass, setting
afire reflections from the mirrors that obliterated the walls. On the
easel, the cloth had been removed from the portrait of him, dressed
in loose-fitting pale trousers and sleeveless pullover on top of a
check shirt open at the neck. He sat sideways on a bench on a lawn
surrounded by summer vegetation. His arm rested on the back of
the bench, the hands were lifted in a gesture of explanation, as he
more than half-turned towards the second portrait of himself in a
full profile that showed clearly the aquiline nose, the thin upper lip
and less thin lower one, dark hair greying at the temples, brushed
back from a high forehead. His arm also rested on the back of the
bench where he sat, but his hands were clasped, listening. In the
middle, behind the central half-turned portrait that hid him below
the neck, was the third portrait of him, full face, looking out of the

canvas through light brown eyes, and smiling though his features were still.

The curtains fluttered in a breeze; trees and shrubs smiled their new leaves; the blaze subsided into ember, and I left the empty room to knock at the tall oak door and look at the beautifully depicted stag before walking around the cloister to greet my beloved and her beloved.

7 The Dome

Afternoon rays slanted through the trees and lit up the undergrowth; Ramyna's grandchild sat a little way from her, blowing soap into bubbles. One big bubble drifted in her direction and before it burst. Ramyna had time to see the iridescent colours and a tiny reflection of herself trapped upside down in glass. It was time to go to the dome, she thought, looking at the lights and strong shadows, the different greens, the sudden splash of yellow of the oak whose leaves always turned early. There was no hurry, she thought, listening to the quarrelling birds and the distant sound of an axe as Nathar and his sons felled branches for winter; but it was time. After the rains she would look for mushrooms and go to the dome. Or perhaps it would be later, after the snows.

Ramyna looked at the familiar trees, the familiar blue sky, the familiar way the rays touched and lit the leaves and their shadows danced on ferns in a slight breeze and followed the familiar track of thought: since she had returned in the year of Tavis' birth, she had experienced a tranquillity inexplicable. What was it? It was not hope that would cause pain if dashed; it had nothing to do with what brought expectation and disappointment. Trust? Trust of what? Yes, maybe there was something that resembled trust, though it was nearer to a knowledge, and she was not sure trust could be described as a knowledge, even if the consequence of such knowledge was trust. It was also indeed hope, Ramyna thought, shaking her head at the difficulty and smiling. But different from any hope she had experienced, or any trust. So different she did not want to use either term.

Her smile broadened for her namesake who climbed into her lap, suddenly in need of comfort; the grandmother enveloped her in her arms, and Ramyna stuck two fingers in her mouth, looking out at the brown squirrels that chased each other from one end of the lawn to the other before disappearing into the beech. Thera rounded the corner into sight, carrying a basket of vegetables, her dome-shaped belly arching her back into an ungainly walk. Ramyna wondered, should she tell Nathar? And immediately regretted the thought. No, of course she would not tell Nathar. Had she not learnt the necessity of secrets? She suspected he knew the dome, but one element in her tranquillity had come from the realization that she would not know anyone, that the search was foolish, as foolish as Tavis' and her own search for a door to the dome when there was no door, as foolish as her search through journeys. Foolish but none the less necessary? Could something be both? It had, after all, been the nameless lover who had taught her her foolishness, and she would never have known him had she not lost Tavis and feared to lose Nathar so that she fled into journeys.

Her granddaughter leapt from her lap and ran indoors after her mother; she could hear their voices, one high-pitched, one low, quiet. Each time she saw the tall, large, fair daughter of her sister, Ramyna was bewildered by her capacity to be. She was like a tree, her mother-in-law thought. A phrase from the book that had been the only gift from her lover that she had kept, came into her head: 'Her ways are ways of pleasantness, and all her paths are peace. She is a tree of life to those who lay hold of her', and she remembered her sister's serenity; her chest tightened in fear that her grand-daughter might resemble her and not her mother. She would never know if she went to the dome, she realized gratefully, as she struggled to her feet and shuffled to meet Nathar and his sons.

When Thera gave birth to Nathar snow had fallen with silent insistence until they had become imprisoned and could not even reach the village. Ramyna helped with the birth of her youngest grandson and while Nathar tended his wife, she paced the room to quieten the newly-born. Was it now complete? she wondered, looking at the minute hands clutched into a fist against the wrinkled face, the tightly shut eyes, the enormous mouth that had just stopped emitting yells too powerful for such smallness and fragility. Or was it about to start again?

Both, she thought, laying the baby in the basket; already he knew how to stretch his small limbs, already two of his fingers found the mouth and his features twitched in sleep. Tavis, Athon and Ramyna gathered to look at him, wide-eyed with tired excitement. It was being recomposed; the stone was turning to show another facet, Ramyna thought. Perhaps now she would be able to go to the dome? She climbed into the narrow cot when Nathar's family was settled, after seeing that the snow-fall had not yet relented: it will, she thought as she fell asleep in the ringing silence of dawn. But she woke a few minutes later from a dream in which she was being dragged and tumbled in the swollen bed of a river, unable to breathe, swallowing water. She had seen her son's head bobbing in the water just above her, his mouth open in a yell she could not hear, and lay rigid in a place she did not recognize while the effects of the dream wore off. Slowly sensation returned, she could move her arms and then her legs, and knew she was lying on her side with her back to the wall and her face towards the hearth where embers still flickered. Must she think about the possible meaning of this dream: she remembered the vision she had had when Nathar was a child, the mouth open in a silent yell. Was there something else to endure, something else to learn? Let it be a meaningless dream, she thought. She was weary of events in her life: the story was too thick, too crowded with possible significances, with possible meaninglessness. Let it be that she find the dome and leave the story to others, better equipped to know the answers or at least not to ask unanswerable questions.

*

Though she was afraid at times during the rest of a relentless winter, and thoughts crowded her mind as insistently as they had since she had first become aware of her knowledge of the dome, behind their quarrelsome whine Ramyna watched her acceptance of whatever was to come, as if there, at the centre, she were already inside the dome, moving about softly within a knowledge that could not yet encompass the area beyond. It did not dull the pain when the dream was realized and Nathar and his daughter were lost in the early spring floods that followed the heavy snows, but it lent the suffering the same dimension of serenity that Thera had: both grieved but were unchanged by the bereavement. How different from her mourning at the loss of Tavis and her terror at the mere thought of the loss of Nathar, that had tossed her into journeys. And yet how necessary it had all been.

Necessary for what? She still wondered, at the moment of spring when no flower had yet died and no leaf was darker than the palest green, and she finally ventured in search of the dome. The ground was soggy and the tracks clogged up with leaves, but the sun shone warm. She walked along the path, distracted into thinking how she recognized every tree; she could tell at the end of winter how many trunks had been uprooted and how many main branches broken under the weight of snow; she knew the landmarks so well she could not fail to take note when they changed, when a bramble died leaving a bald patch, or there was a burst of growth and the ground that the previous year had been bracken was carpeted with violets and anemones and bluebells. She counted the trees she had seen grow from barely noticed seedling to saplings, to mature ash, oak, plane, beech, hazelnut, cedar, chestnut, dogwood, larch, elm, syca-more, walnut: Ramyna named them all, fingering the words as if she were handling silk. How naturally they exist, she thought, envious of their immutability through every change. Year after year they had followed the necessary route of change. Necessary why? Perhaps there was no reason, just as there was no reason why the dome existed. It existed to give reason for something else to exist, perhaps? Could trees exist simply to give pleasure? How desolate it would be for a tree to exist without anyone perceiving its existence and wondering at its beauty and presence. Ramyna stopped to grapple with the thought before it vanished and became suddenly aware of the mass of sound and of how she could distinguish each instrument, breeze brushing leaves, water tumbling over low ridges, birds competing for mates with full-throated enthusiasm. They existed, but did not know. Thera existed, but had never reflected on her existence: her strength came from not knowing, from being unreflecting surface that could be encircled, defined, ringed like a tree. She was close to the dome, Ramyna realized: she had never been along this avenue of elms whose leaves smiled silver light. She

herself however was image and reflection, she could not be, but
had to reflect being, she had at each moment to create herself by
questioning. To think and to reflect: words that demanded reflection
of her, like close and closed, like truth containing concealment. She
had to think, to reflect or she would cease to exist, as the image in
a mirror ceases to exist when out of the beam of reflection.

Oh, she had wanted to be Thera; she still wished she had been,
to continue, immutable as a tree through every change: like water,
like birds, like trees, Thera would be replaced when the time came,
by someone blessedly like her, immutable as a tree through every
change. But it was also true, Ramyna thought as the avenue opened
out and the top of the dome dazzled her with its light, it was also
true that only her own existence, her reflecting existence, could give
a shape to the unreflecting existence of a tree, of Thera. It was her
knowledge of the dome that gave it all meaning, that recreated life
as something with purpose—even if the purpose was merely to make
her aware of reflection and the unreflecting existence. How tiring
to hold that thought, to face the shimmering reflection of the word
and hold it steady in her mind: it dissembled, leaving her both
elated and strangely sad. It was also true, she persisted as she
removed her shoes to walk once more barefoot in the grass and
approach the dome, it was also true that she had imposed a knowledge on Tavis that destroyed them, and had imagined, invented a
knowledge for Athon and Nathar: she had wanted them to be with
her in the struggle to be and had not accepted that their existence
was like Thera's, like the trees, that she was alone with the burden
of thought, the elation of knowledge and the terror of reflection; the
terror of thought and knowledge, the elation of reflection.

The dome was dazzling: someone had been tending it. The
restored beds swayed with flowers that bowed towards the dome,
as if looking at themselves in the mirrors. Butterflies fluttered from
one to the other and against the dome surface in vain attempts to
reach the reflection of flowers. Ramyna pushed the door and it
immediately gave way. The hall exactly mimicked the home she
and Tavis had had. The fire in the large hearth at one end cast a
warm light full of shadows on the oak table, the cupboard and the
rocking chair. As she approached it, she recognized utensils and
crockery hanging above the fireplace. On the smaller table next to-

the rocking-chair was the lamp she had always lit when Tavis drew the curtains. With the lamp was a volume bound in cloth, decorated with colourful geometric patterns. She saw when she flicked through it that the writing changed a number of times and the last pages were blank. Ramyna laid it down and moved slowly, touching now this, now that object. All memory contained in objects, she thought. All life in the choice of what to furnish life with. She remembered the care they had taken and remembered their love in that care. In one corner, close to the hearth, was the cradle; at the opposite end their bed, heavy, large, dark with blankets. Ramyna stretched herself on it and looked up into the vault; at night, the roof of the cabin would be invisible, and its beams would sometimes surprise her when a flicker from the dying fire caught them for a fraction, as if they came to sudden life. Whenever it happened, she would dwell on the dome, as if there were some connection between it and that momentary illumination. Yet as she lay on the bed she still could not grasp what the connection was, although the same strange sensation—or perhaps its memory—came to her. But the vault of the dome was too high, and Ramyna rose, lit the lamp with twigs from the container on the mantel and sat, rocking gently, waiting for her husband and her son, and expecting her brother.

*

She didn't know how long she sat in absence of thought before she began to wonder what was in the volume, the only unfamiliar object in the room. She picked the book up and traced the colour mazes with her finger. Is it necessary, she asked the dome: she was reluctant to open the book, it was unyielding and heavy and the effort of lifting her hand to turn the pages was too great. She was tired, she thought. It was not the weariness of thought. Her bones were tired. She would skim through the book, then lay herself out on the bed and wait. She turned to the contents page: the four titles leapt at her. Of course, she thought with a catch in her throat, it had to be. How else could she know them, she thought as she looked at the epigraph in bold black italic 'In a glass darkly . . . face to face . . .'

She no longer felt tired: she carried the lamp to the table, where she sat and turned to read the first, Athon's story. While she read

the lamp became unecessary as the light grew denser with rays
from the rising sun. She could hear outside their home the sound
of Nathar's laugh and Tavis' chuckle. She knew that when she lifted
her eyes from the page the dew on the grass would be shining like
splintered glass and she would see them engaged in some chore
that was a game for the child. She knew that Athon had gone deep
into the forest and would be back at nightfall. She knew that though
four stories were finished, the blank pages were for her story. She
paused in her reading long enough to flick through and write the
first lines on the first empty page, then she smiled and turned back
the pages where she could know the dome was a function of dreams,
and it was dreams that made them all real.

ABOUT THE AUTHOR

M. J. Fitzgerald was born in New York in 1950 and lived in Italy from the age of three until she was sent to school in England in 1964. She received a B.A. from Sussex University and a B.Phil. from York University. She has worked as a free-lance publisher's reader and translator as well as teaching part time in Tutorial Colleges and Adult Education Institutes. Between September 1984 and September 1985 she was Southern Arts Writer-in-Residence in Southampton, England. She is also the author of a novel, *Concertina.*